TALL SHOT STORIES

(A picture book for adults)
(Including the UNTDC series)

TALL SHOT STORIES

(A picture book for adults)
(Including the UNTDC series)

Ruster Keaton

First Step Publishing
Paving Ways For New Writers

First Published in 2018 by First Step Publishing
Editorial / Sales / Marketing Office at
303-304 Garnet Nirmal Lifestyles Ph 2
Behind Nirmal Lifestyles Mall
LBS Marg Mulund West
Mumbai 400080
E-Mail:- info@firststepcorp.com
www.firststepcorp.com

ISBN:- 978-93-83306-43-5
Cover Designed by: Design Fishing
Price: INR 650 India and Rest USD 30

Dedicated to:

My loving wife Mallika

Bush

Dumpy, Fur Ball, Dumps, Pachhdupa, Muchhad Kaka, Powder Puff, Squeesh Ball, Tumoo Baba, Roll in One

Caramel, Russian Bear, Orange Eyes

Birdies

(H)Olly, Almond Beauty

& Chintu, 4 month old, Blacku Mama, Bear, Sphinxy, Pudsy, Garfield, Chintu 2, Chintu 3, Mintu, Lame Spot, White Angels, Blackie 2, Spotty, and Blackie 1.

Stories

personal favorites of Ruster Keaton

Wanted – Dead or Oiled

Fadi Meshan squinted into the blazing afternoon Texas sun. He was quite at home in the desert; he had been born in and to the desert, a Bedouin at heart. A major part of his life had been spent in the southern Arabian peninsula where he learnt to ride. Fadi could ride, in fact he could ride just about anything that had four legs and a tail. He'd ridden horses, camels, donkeys, an elephant, a zebra and with some mixed success a young giraffe, but that was a long time ago and the giraffe had forgiven him, he was young. It was said that he was a whisperer, could talk, no, the correct was to describe it was 'speak' with animals. He had a ranch now in Texas, over four to six thousand head of good quality breeding cattle, a stockade of close to sixty top quality free range mustangs, around two dozen floating riding horses and at least four good racing colts. The farm also maintained its share of poultry, geese, donkeys (two pets and some load bearing), and around three dozen mulch cows, over fifty goats; no pigs was the only concession to his faith. Fadi's ranch was all of nearly three hundred and fifty miles wide and around 33 miles in length, watered with streams and two mid-sized fresh water lakes, splitting at the seams with trout.

He could not have wanted more. The main ranch house was built at the north end with a slopping hillock around two hundred meters off to the right and the easy corrals on the left. Chuck station was put up immediately behind the house. It was a comfortable house, and it did not need to be luxurious. Al Meshan was a good shot, actually good with both a handgun and the rifle. He was at home with the Colt .45, the shotgun, the Winchester repeater and the Sharps buffalo. He preferred the Colt P1870, which was slightly long barreled, allowing for better accuracy. Fadi always maintained that a Colt was no good if you could not shoot the eyeballs off a rattler at fifty feet, or trim the end of a match at twenty feet. Speed meant zip, accuracy was everything in the West. The P1870 was longer in the tooth and took a low slung open ended holster, not ideal for riding, however, when riding, Fadi always had the Winchester in the boot.

He really liked his weapons, cared for them, had them in sets of four, although he only used one Colt and the one Winchester at any one time. Fadi was good with the Colt but really good with the Winchester. He could put a parting in the hair of a bear at two hundred meters, and in fact once did. Ranch hands still get a look at the bear with the funny parting hairstyle down the center. Fadi Meshan was a hunter and a trader. He had been a hunter and trader in Arabia and was one in Texas. Selling gold, spices, trading horses, and travelling for over a year he finally reached North America in 1895. He was also a bounty hunter and a rogue Red Indian hunter when he felt so inclined. The Governor and the local sheriffs had paid out more reward money to Fadi than they cared to remember. He brought in bodies by the cartload some weekends, all stacked four high, and neatly arranged, rogue Red Indians out front, red necks to the rear, the 'wanted' notices neatly pinned to their vests. Nobody liked the Arab but I, Governor Bancockk had nothing to show that Fadi had ever done anything wrong. Almost all of the corpses had neat bullet holes, front to back, dead center of the forehead or chest, some .45s some .44s and one or two with fist size holes in the chest from the Sharp. And Fadi never took scalps, he respected the dead.

I looked Fadi over quietly, twirling the right end of my moustache "You're probably wondering why I've called you here, Fadi. Fact is we need a bit of help. We have over 250 counties and its gets so darn tacky. Law and order simply isn't what it used to be. We have a bit of a problem down at Beaumont. Bunch of Mexicans raking up trouble, at Spindletop Hill" "Send in the Rangers, Guv" Fadi threw back at me. He was nobody's hired gun so far and was not about to begin. Fadi knew that being a hired gun for the Governor was one step away from a pardon, two steps away from the outlaw trail on the run, and three steps away from a fat noose. "Can't do, Fadi" I ruminated sipping my coffee. It was thick coffee and while it would not float a horseshoe, it certainly floated something in it, maybe a dash of chili, I thought idly. "Fresh out of smart Rangers, this needs somebody with a head, a steady gun hand and nobody from around there. Trouble is, Fadi, I don't understand what's going on. Too much smoke in the air". "Isn't Spindletop the bubbling gas salt field? Fadi pitched in. "Thought so too, but these Mexicans and two gents Higgins and Lucas don't think so. Think the place is sitting on a massive oil field". "Talk about letting sitting or sleeping dogs lie" Fadi grinned. He was not too old to enjoy the lighter side, and at 36 he still had traces of Arabic humor.

"Well, Okkaay" reluctantly Fadi agreed "I'll give it a shot....or two or three". "Good man" I said, cheering up a bit "Here's the folder on the problem, a nice thick envelope of expense money, a new identity (won't do to have you riding around as a newly minted gun slinging Arab immigrant) and some posters". "Posters? Fadi looked both worried and surprised. "Sure" I grinned "You're the new wanted man, got to be convincing, you're not going to get anything done unless they're scared stiff of you". "What's wrong with using Jim Green (aka the Texas outlaw 'Sudden' as recounted by Oliver Strange) or one of ole Devil Hardin's floating outfit for this job then?" Fadi queried, now a bit suspicious. "Jim's a bit partial to shooting up Mexicans or Indians and Dusty's men are busy on some fool outlaw trail off Laredo". "How much for expenses and what's the new id and the posters say?" Fadi queried now leafing through the folder". "Five hundred dollars on expenses and your new identity is Bruce C. Rudy" I grinned adding "like the name? I love christenings".

Fadi walked out and set about getting himself geared up. He went down to the nearest printer and on the Governor's account asked for a hundred copies of the poster to be printed by four that evening, and planned to leave town for Spindletop that evening. Later that afternoon Fadi, all dressed in a black outfit, looking like a grim reaper gun slinger, picked up the posters and set out for Beaumont. He rode a quiet but hardy sorrel, tagged along a faster grey Morgan horse named Bullrain and two mules for loads, a virtual little caravan but no real company. Fadi was used to desert hikes on his own and was good at survival, in fact he was a threat to anybody or anything he encountered when he was on a hunt. The Morgan had cost him a packet and saved him a dozen packets. On a chase, the grey had never yet let him down, always faster, more durable than anything he had chased. Jim Green he heard preferred a paint horse for its nimbleness but in his line of work, Fadi leant toward speed and endurance.

On the way to Beaumont, Fadi distributed the posters. The posters had a fair picture likeness of him, and mentioned that he was wanted alive by Governor Bancockk with a reward of four thousand dollars, briefly describing him as armed and dangerous. His name however was misspelt in the posters. In the rush to give him the posters by four that afternoon, the printer had put in a name of Brent Crude instead of Brent C. Rudy. Fadi shrugged it off, what difference did it make anyway? The picture was good, and the description was good for the job too.

I was vaguely worried. It had been three, no four months since I had met with Fadi and while Spindletop had since been quiet, there had been no news at all from Fadi. So I was pleasantly surprised when Ah Kum, my Chinese secretary announced that a Mr. Brent Crude was there to see me. It was 1899 and I was keen to retire with a cheery song. I observed him carefully as he walked to

11

the door. I knew that time was running out but suppressed the urge to check my watch. I took a deep breath and started counting in reverse under my breath. "Ten, nine, eight, seven..."Fadi stepped in. I was stunned at the transformation "Tell me" was all I could muster. "Didn't have to fire a bullet after all" Fadi grinned, looking younger than his 36 and now dressed in a linen suit and a bowler hat. "The Mexicans were right. Spindletop is sitting on a large bucket of oil. We got together at the corral and simply hammered out a deal. The Mexicans are funding the drilling, through a company in Pittsburgh in exchange for forty percent of the oil rights. Local man named Lucas gets to keep only one eighth of the shares. And they've given me twenty percent, all signed, sealed and notary delivered. Here's fifty dollars and change with a receipt for the balance expenses and stuff" Fadi concluded. "So, are you now Brent or Fadi? I asked, not knowing what to make of all this and a little at a loss. "Brent Crude of course, it's a nice name, a rich name. But I am planning to go back home and look to see if I can sprout some oil there as well. This oil gig looks very promising" Fadi tipped his hat and ducked out of my offices, got aboard his very own coach waiting outside and that was the last I saw of the Arab gun slinger. Oil was discovered at Spindletop in 1901 (the biggest ever gusher in North America), Iran in 1911, Bahrain in 1932 and Saudi Arabia in 1938. Beaumont is still looking for a wanted criminal called Brent Crude and Fadi somewhere above is playing the markets.

The Horns of The Dilemma – Aunt Fritzy

Anybody who has seen the political map of Africa, and given it some thought will chuckle. Clearly, somebody had played a cruel joke on the continent, drawing horizontal or vertical lines across latitude and longitude with a great degree of latitude. Wayne Braithwhite was born in Madagascar. Wayne was adventurous and since an early age wanted to explore the world, wanted much more than the island's lemurs, snails and chameleons had to offer by way of development. The first human settlements were said to have occurred in Madagascar around 450 BC, (the canoeing visitors from Borneo) and on many days, young Wayne opined that the lemurs and chameleons were definitely smarter than the locals, whereas the snails had adapted superbly to the pace of local life.

At the young age of 12, Wayne left Madagascar. Wayne fudged his age on some papers, took a job pulling rope on a boat (an assorted goods freighter) and left. The poor boy did not set foot on land again, except for the loading and unloading events, for over fourteen months and when he did, he discovered that they were in Valletta, Malta. On the way, Wayne had handled, pitched, loaded, unloaded chirping birds, chattering monkeys, colorful parrots, fruit, canned peaches and mushrooms, innumerable sacks of flour, two baby giraffes (Naja and Enad), one caged and very upset leopard, tons of salt, tons of washing soap and floated he thought a billion logs of wood to the shoreline. He would not be seriously disappointed if he never again saw a sack of flour in his life.

Wayne had lived for two whole months shoveling grass to the giraffes and he had briefly disembarked at Zanzibar, Kismayu off Somalia and Djibouti. He had been ill with a fever for some time and was out cold when the freighter stopped off at a few other places along the way. Captain Jon Wesnip was a South African who was good at command, an excellent sailor and a very astute trader. Jon had run the East Africa – Horn to Malta route for years and knew perfectly well where he could buy the flour, the monkeys, parrots (and where he could sell them) – although, even he would admit that the giraffes were not really planned for. The occasional leopard got its ticket up north, but that was a rare occurrence to, as leopards are not particularly good at sea, despite what anybody from Noah's ark may have to say about it. Jon would have sworn that this leopard was at one point so ill that its spots changed around to yellow and black from black and yellow.

Valletta could not hold Wayne's interest much longer. Wayne stayed but a few dozen weeks in Valletta before he set off on another freighter headed for East Africa. Some months and two fevers later, Wayne reached Mombassa. Even the vastness of the sea could not compare with the vastness of Africa. East Africa quite simply rolled on, and on, for miles of tall grass lands, hills and lakes, actually one massive lake. Wayne loved Kenya. He spent time fishing at Nakuru, learnt to caddy for British golfers at the picturesque El Doret club, and picked tea leaves on the slopes. Wayne worked for a while too at Mara Sarena helping the forest rangers but thought it too dangerous. Oh, he had seen his fair share of danger while on the freighter with Captain Wesnip but Wayne did not consider tracking lions a risk – he thought it was a simple attempt at suicide, as in those days, the rangers only carried a stout stick and a lantern. Wayne tried hard but it was impossible to befriend any of the family of the pride of lions he was tracking. The friendliest little fellow, named Ralphie, not yet a year old, lost Wayne's heart and interest when he saw him tearing into the belly of a live, struggling fawn, ripping out the insides with streams of blood gushing around his little whiskers.

Wayne was bored. East Africa and the lions and grasslands were a risk, but a boring risk. Nothing really exciting ever happened, and when it did, it inevitably resulted in a death, a gory messy death, like being bored by a rhino or trampled by a bull elephant or being run over by a scampering herd of zebra. So it was not with some reluctance that Wayne made his way back to Captain Jon Wesnip when he next came around after a few months, to Mombasa. 'Had enough of sight-seeing, wot? Wesnip quipped, half glad to see the steady hand back, for he was always short-handed, losing crew faster than he could recruit.

'Have you heard of the Golden Hoof? The Captain asked with a straight face, giving away nothing. 'Vaguely, Capn' Wayne replied 'but I don't really know anything other than its supposed to be a pure gold hoof the size of a small hillock somewhere in East Africa'. 'Not somewhere, we know exactly where' Wesnip replied 'We're being funded an expedition, putting together a two hundred man crew to get it out. Wages and profits for all'. 'Wages AND profit ? Wayne perked up, now interested. But this was after all in East Africa, he knew the place, how difficult could it be. 'Have to rig up the old boat a bit, Wayne, will take two or three months, but you will work with us and on full wages'. So Wayne joined the team. The freighter was now carrying a green, red and black flag with a white crossed moon on the top right end of the flag. Wesnip explained that the freighter and the whole expedition was being paid for by and Arab named Louay Al Ajeel. Louay was the 14th son of an Arab Sheikh and clearly as the 14th son, his route to wealth involved investing a bit in risky ventures. Louay was all of 24 years old, but a fair marksman, a good swordsman and an amazing horseman.

The Antoinne [for that was the name of the freighter now] moved out of the prying eyes of Mombasa, stopped briefly for supplies off the black hills of Kilifi before pulling up a small river at Malindi. The Antoinne was docked dry and the outfitting began. Wayne first developed pangs of worry when he saw that the changes in fact were rapidly transforming The Antoinne into a canon equipped fighting ship. The freighter was broken down for speed, the anchors made heavy for quick stops, the rudder and sails strengthened. Cargo decks were stripped and racks of weapons, swords, spears, cutlasses and muskets were added. An ammunition room was added, musket balls and powder kegs and piles of heavy canon shot, buckets of dry tar and drums of nails. They were going into battle!!! Captain Wesnip was busy it seemed and simply did not have time to talk. There were men all over the place, doing a hundred things all at once. Three months later The Antoinne was unrecognizable. The sheep had been transformed into a wolf with teeth and a nasty temperament. Somehow the crew did not very much like the given name and soon everybody, for some reason was calling the ship Aunt Fritzy.

Captain Wesnip gave the orders and Aunt Fritzy with some fanfare pulled out of Malindi. All signs of habitation at the camp were emptied, carted away or simply burnt down. When they set sail Aunt Fritzy had nearly 300 fighting men on board, having said that, everybody (including the cooks) could both fight and cook bread and chicken !!. Days of quiet sailing began. Captain Wesnip did most of his sailing at night, laying up the ship on corners of the river during the daylight hours. The river was calm, the surface ruffled only by the occasional crocodile. One crocodile, Wayne named Brother Fritz followed them for three whole days, watching them when they dropped anchor and swimming alongside when they moved after dusk. Brother Fritz was easily over 30 feet in length and at his waist five or six feet in width with the nicest row of teeth, Wayne had ever seen in East Africa (including Ralphie – for some reason Wayne still worried about little Raphie hunting all by himself).

Wesnip's mood darkened as they grew nearer to their objective. They passed the Tsava Voi, headed up toward Kibwezi before Wesnip announced that in two days they would anchor off Machakos from where they would make their way inland on foot. The jungle was now thick around them. This was not grassland or tea plantation area. They were still in East Africa hundreds of kilometers away from the Masai Steppe (and far away from Ralphie). Once they reached Machakos matters took a turn for the worse very rapidly. It seemed that the legend of the Golden Hoof shaped hillock was true. What was not well advertised was that the area was protected by warriors from the nearby Kitui, Murang'a, and Thika tribes.

These were hunter tribes who believed in the whole tradition of poison arrows, poison frogs, poison snakes, crocodile heads, painted bodies and their protection by a phantom who lived in a skull cave and rode a white horse. Shinegwa who was head of the Kitui tribe and the elder of the war council had heard of the war vessel coming in and the stories of the threat to the Golden Hoof. Shinegwa was originally from a Japanese Samurai family which had settled in East Africa some two hundred years earlier. He knew a bit about battle craft and was not worried about Aunt Fritzy. Captain Wesnip on the other hand, had no knowledge that the tribes were led by somebody of Shinegwa's skills in battle. Shinwega had around a hundred warriors armed with spears and poison arrows, and he sent for more warriors from the tribes of Limuru and Kericho. Nakuru warriors wanted to join but Shinwega held them off, knowing they were too head strong and would not work as a team.

Twelve of Wesnip's scouts set off toward Machakos, leaving Aunt Fritzy on small paddle boats, four to a boat. Four days later two scouts returned, half running, half walking, one with an arrow in his shoulder (he died a painful death two days later). It had been a rout. The scouts had been captured alive, tortured, stripped, eaten alive and what was left was fed to a relative of Brother Fritz. At least one of the tribes quite definitely had a palate for human flesh, live, squirming, freshly cut human flesh. Shinegwa did not approve of cannibalism but he could not muzzle his warriors. Wesnip considered the situation and his options. Wesnip was not a battle commander but he did not give up easily and had seen his fair share of trouble. So it was that on the morning of the third day after the scouts had returned (Shinegwa's warriors clearly did not have the courage to storm Aunty Fritzy), the ship's canons opened up, six to the side, broad siding the land fall before the ship. The foliage was ripped by blazing balls of tar, exploding balls of hot nails overhead and huge explosions that ripped the trees from their roots, flattening hillocks. Hour after hour the heavy guns boomed burning the land, leaving embers and ashes in the wake of the canon shot. The sky was darkened with smoke, the only sound was the rhythmic thumping of the canon, the whistle of the canon shot and the hot blast as the balls struck.

Wesnip took risks but calculated risks. He was at the core a trader. The canon continued for a second day. This time Aunt Fritzy moved slightly in shore giving it greater range. Then planks were lowered and four canon were taken ashore blasting a path in front of it. On the third day of the explosions, the crew began getting on shore with an assortment of battle gear, spears, shields, cutlasses, swords, axes and even chain balls. Two hundred paid, would-be assassins readied the land assault for the Golden Hoof at Machakos, now covered ahead by six canon, something that Shinegwa did not have. The Kitui tribe was placed as the last barrier at the Golden Hoof. These were supposedly the fiercest warriors. Shinegwa formed an advance party of the Thika with the Murang'a being used to support as reserves.

Wesnip's forces, now known as the Fritzers first encountered the Thika on an open field, a few miles south of Machakos. Over 200 of Wesnips' fighting crew met the Thika head on. The Thika were outnumbered. Some said there were 20, some said 50, but they were outnumbered at least four to one and it was a losing fight to begin with. The hungry, savage, angry Thika could not match the greed and fear of the Fritzers, who were mortally afraid of losing, being captured alive and eaten alive. The savage battle took but an hour and not more than eight or ten Thika left the place running, the rest were slaughtered. Over 30 Thika lay dead in the field, cut to pieces, the Fritzers taking what trophies they could (here they were lucky as the Thika wore their prized possessions into battle). Wesnip was not bothered with the body count but counted all the same because he needed to know how many Fritzers he had left. Wesnip was quickly working out larger profit shares (and his own) with each reduction in his crew!! At the battle with the Thika, the Thika's 30 warriors had cost Wesnip fifty five men, forty two dead and thirteen seriously injured, and likely to die, there being not much by way of medical treatment. Anyway, the seriously injured would be unable to take part in any further proceedings, so they were headed back to Aunt Fritzy where Wayne suspected they would eventually wind up as food for Brother Fritz. Wayne himself had been safe. He had been working as Wesnip's assistant of sorts for a while now and did not take part in the fighting.

Jawad Otaba the leader of the Murang'a force had been watching carefully. He noted that the Fritzers fought with gusto, fear and greed, always a potent combination in a fighting force. Jawad also noted that the Fritzers had advance canon firmly established to support them in the initial skirmish and around 250 fighting men. The Murang'a were just about ninety and did not have any powder, canon or muskets. The Murang'a were good shots with arrows and handy with spears. The Murang'a were accustomed to eating a hearty meal before a battle and unlike the Thika left their prized possessions with their families and young sons not yet fifteen. They painted their upper bodies a strange fluorescent blue. After the defeat of the Thika, Shinegwa's leadership came under some scrutiny and for a couple of days Shinegwa was not heard of. The Fritzers headed further north inland toward their goal, now marching confidently, some singing, their mood quite upbeat. Another day and they would be at the foot of the Golden Hoof. Within hours of their march through the thick forest on the second day, they could see the Golden Hoof.

It was a hoof shaped hillock, a copper brownish color with a winding trail up one side and a temple like structure at the top. A sprinkling of warriors at the foot around the Hoof (these were the Kitui) appeared on guard but nothing of worry to the Fritzers. If anything, this guard was even smaller than the Thika force they had encountered earlier. The men principally began discussing between themselves how much gold they could carry back to Aunt Fritzy. Musket balls were loaded but Wesnip decided not to use canon so near the Golden Hoof. The Fritzers decided to make camp, pitch tents, settle in, plan a bit, study the lay of the land, work out a direct route, eat a bit, rest up a bit and make merry a while. It was around four in the afternoon after their meal when the men were drowsy and happy when the Murang'a force struck the camp.

Jawad Otaba, Wayne noted later in his diary, led the force. They entered the camp and ran through it. Tens of dozens of blue warriors raced through the camp slashing and setting on fire as they went. It was over in a few minutes, maybe fifteen or twenty. Then suddenly they were gone. Otaba had held back thirty men and once his fighters had run through the camp, they let loose with arrows. The sky was darkened as a hail of poison arrows hit the camp, some lit with fire, shredding what life was left in the camp. The Kitui watched with interest from a distance. At the corner of the foothill Shinegwa sat on a ragged brown pony, spear in hand, impassively watching the action, slightly pleased when he saw the follow up with the arrows. The Fritzers were wiped out. Beside Shinegwa sitting bare backed on a greyish white horse, sat a masked man in dark blue, with what looked like a wolf sitting at the feet of the horse. The Murang'a and the Kitui immediately recognized the Phantom. The legend said he could defeat a bull elephant and that he was the immortal guardian of the East, living in a skull shaped cave. Wesnip had rushed out to defend himself at the first charge. He went down later under the hail of arrows, taken in the leg by a poison arrow. So it came that the adjutant Wayne Braithwhite became along with around twenty others, prisoners of the Murang'a.

Wayne was relieved it was the Murang'a and not the Thika but decided they would be soon killed in some gruesome manner. Brother Fritz, he figured must be smacking his lips at the forthcoming meals. Shinegwa and the phantom decided not to take further part. The captives were herded into a holding area. Jawad Otaba decided that the only good and pleasing way to deal with the captives would be to feed them to the animals. An enclosure was set up, some four square miles within sight of the Golden Hoof. Wayne was later told that some animals including a lion, rhino and giraffe were herded in the area. For days the captives were let into the enclosure in pairs and the tribes cheered on as one or more of the animals tore the captives, limb to limb, with a pack of hyenas finishing off the remains.

Three or four days into the festivities it was Wayne's turn. Wayne was led out into the enclosure together with another Fritzer who called himself Gorman. Gorman lasted about four or five minutes, eventually ending up with his body smashed to pieces by a furious giraffe. The first kick had shattered his ribs, the second had knocked his brains out in a soggy greyish, reddish brown mess on to the ground and then the other giraffe proceeded to stomp him into the ground. The rhino never really got into the action, the lions were not yet to be seen but the hyenas did a clean job of the finishing. Wayne ventured out, calm now, he had no illusions. The lead giraffe who was quicker rushed forward and then screeched to a halt a mere few feet from Wayne. The giraffe leaned down and purred, growled. The second giraffe thundered in and stood off to one side puzzled then charged, then halted, the growled and braked again. Wayne had just met up again with Najla and Enad his two babies who remembered.

Meanwhile the rhino appeared on the edge of the clearing and the giraffes backed away. The rhino was around a hundred meters away. He lowered his head and thundered in. The very ground shaking under then as the four ton beast charged, tossing his head from side to side. Another few minutes and it would now definitely be over.

Suddenly, there was a roar from behind Wayne. To add to his troubles, a massive mangy, much scarred and nasty looking lion leapt into the clearing. Wayne side stepped, in seconds the lion and the rhino were face to face. The rhino braked his charge into a screeching halt, a cloud of dust thrown up. Suddenly he had lost interest, turned and the ground shaking as he jogged away. Wayne was left looking at the lion now fifty feet away from him. Nowhere to hide, nowhere to run. The lion walked up to Wayne, alternately snarling and purring, showing his teeth and warily looking around and behind Wayne. The pair of giraffe were moving back in, not as afraid of the lion, but still wary. The lion lay down and rolled on to his back for a belly rub. And so it was that Wayne had just met up again with little Ralphie, only not so little now.

Jawad Otaba's Murang'a, and the Thika had been trying for a while to rid themselves of Shinegwa. They kept him on only because it seemed he had the support of the Phantom, the Guardian of the East. But it was the Murang'a who had defeated the Fritzers and the Thika who had made the first sacrifices. Selecting a new leader had been a problem because the new leader could be from the Thika, Murang'a, Kitui or even the Limuru and Kericho tribes. The war council had decided to retire Shinegwa who it was said went off to live in the skull cave with the phantom, his greyish white horse and wolf. The coalition, compromise leader of the war council was the new comer Wayne Braithwhite whom the very animals feared and worshipped. The tribes had never had such a leader. Wayne was renamed Akura Hayet for 'fierce one' in Kitui dialect.

And so Akura Hayet was the first popularly elected guardian of the East, and the first official park ranger of the tribes. Akura used Aunt Fritzy (Akura eventually renamed it The Wesnip and the trading post was known, still is known as Wesnip's trading post) for trading up and down, between the Machakos and Kibwezi. The Golden Hoof lay untouched and is still there to this very day. Brother Fritz was fed with goats and lived to be over a hundred (years old and feet in length) but is no longer there. The Murang'a were trained in horsemanship and Akura never bothered with the Phantom and his wolf. Ralphie, Enad and Najla lived to ripe old ages. The Murang'a sell the choicest poison arrow head to mercenaries at Wesnip's trading post, the Kitui sell the best jungle brew (rumours are that international space station cosmonauts always take a bottle with them). Around 1850, the Thika started preparing a choice chicken and liver grilled dish. It eventually made its way to India, taken there by the trader Louay Al Ajeel. In India the grilled spicy chicken nuggets were called Chicken Tikka (which is today one of the best-selling dishes in the United Kingdom, actually a dish originally based on live human liver gravy). The Golden Hoof itself lost its importance and interest when it was eventually discovered that the hillock was copper and not gold after all. It is now overgrown with grass and Raphie's descendants hunt wildebeest and zebra at the foothills. Akura himself lived to the age of 143 eventually ironically being gored by a rhino not far from the Wesnip Trading post.

A Twist in the Tale

'What the hell is going on between my husband and that bitch?' Maya's patience was at its lowest ebb and she was ready to burst. Sanjay knew that she was serious 'Look, Maya. There is nothing going on between the two of them. Just a little bit of healthy flirting, I'd say. 'Flirting? Healthy flirting? Really Sanjay.' she rolled her eyes in disgust. 'That's what you men call it? There is nothing healthy about flirting, Sanjay, not for a married man. Healthy flirting is a term introduced by perverted men who want to lend legitimacy to their extramarital dalliances. Flirting invariably has a sexual connotation to it.' She got up from her seat and walked around the room gesticulating and muttering something to herself. Suddenly she stopped, turned back, looked at Sanjay and asked, 'Did my husband sleep with her? You are his friend. Did he ever tell you anything about it?'

Maya and Piyush, her husband of fourteen years had settled in Kansas. Piyush had become hugely successful in his electronics hardware business, acquiring along the way a few houses, horses, offices, fancy cars, and yes, some 'friends'. 'He's changed so much, Sanjay, really, I don't know him anymore. He sleeps separately in the guest room....in

31

fact, I don't even know when he sleeps. For the past six months, it's like I've been living with a stranger.' Sanjay looked disturbed trying to calm Maya down and not half succeeding 'Patience, Maya, don't jump the gun, probably nothing to it, its harmless, I know Piyush better, he can't change all that much.' 'I've had it, Sanjay' Maya shrieked 'It's over!! I've tolerated this long enough, he just doesn't care enough anymore to even try and make it work, he does not even bother going through the motions. He just stayed at office on my last birthday, remember…...' Maya wasn't given to crying but she was now embarrassingly (for Sanjay) close to breaking down.

Sanjay looked crestfallen. He had been close to Piyush long since they had come to the USA from back home in Sri Nagar Extension, Gurgaon. They were close knit then, good, solid, green tea, organic families. There had been time for breakfast together, reading the newspapers in the morning, and then dinner or a snack together after six. They even knew the name of the newspaper boy. Everybody knew what was happening in everybody's home (they lived then in homes, not houses, and it was there was warmth, and good natured gossip). He knew where this was heading. Maya had always been 'modern', ahead of the game, and in a very potent combination, Maya was headstrong too. And that was how Piyush and Maya were married despite Maya being a Gujarati with a sweet tooth, and Piyush from a traditional red chili loving Rajasthani Marwari family. Maya was the anti-thesis of the Marwari perception of Gujarati's. Maya was a veritable, horse over the wall Rani of Jhansi, valor over judgment being her motto.

Sanjay looked grimly at Maya 'I really think you are taking this too seriously. We are in Kansas but even here men do not love their dogs (bitch in this case) so much, Maya. Granted he pets her, talks to her, sleeps with her, spends most of his free time exercising or shampooing her or cuddling her, but you can't start thinking he has given you up for a dog !! 'Bitch, not dog' Maya corrected angrily 'And, I've put up with it for long enough. Jenny means more to him than anything else. He even changed his office and business hours to spend more time with her!! As for sleeping with her, the way things are in Kansas, they will soon probably get a license to marry too. I wish them luck, but I WILL find a way to teach Piyush a lesson, that stupid, dog, no, bitch …. It's just sick, I tell you, it's beyond sick. If I knew things would come to this here, I would have stayed my whole life in Sri Nagar Extension.' 'Well, at least it's a bitch and not a dog' Sanjay said trying to comfort Maya, and that was when she screamed at him and threw the cup at him with the saucer for company.

Four months later, Sanjay was sitting at a Starbunks, sipping a confusionio with his good friend Piyush. 'So, did the divorce come through, all done and dandy? 'Yes' Piyush grinned with his 24 carat seventy two mm smile 'all done'. 'We had some tough divorce negotiations,

Maya wanted to make me miserable.' 'What did she get, then? Sanjay asked 'half of everything or more? 'Well, she really, really wanted to hurt me Sanjay' Piyush said quietly with a straight face 'so she took from me the one thing closest to me, letting me keep everything else, and besides she really does not need the money.' There was a moment of silence. Then Sanjay burst out laughing 'She took the bitch Jenny, didn't she??!! 'Yes' Piyush was laughing aloud now, heartily 'She fell for it, Sanjay. I had her convinced that the bitch Jenny was the closest thing to me ever, forever. I really can't stand dog hair and saliva; you know the problems I had in Sri Nagar Extension. And' here Piyush almost doubled up laughing 'she joked to her friends that it looked as if I wanted to marry the bitch!!! 'So you have all your money intact, my friend? Sanjay queried delicately. 'Of course' Piyush roared 'she actually threw the asset list in my face and stormed out of the room asking only for Jenny'. 'Alright then' Sanjay smiled a quite smile of satisfaction and contentment 'Piyush, we've got a county clerk not seven miles from here who will issue us a marriage license'. They finished their confusionios and walked out hand in hand, Sanjay took the wheel, and after all he had been (is) the driving force in their relationship anyway.

Yellowstone Frozen Dessert

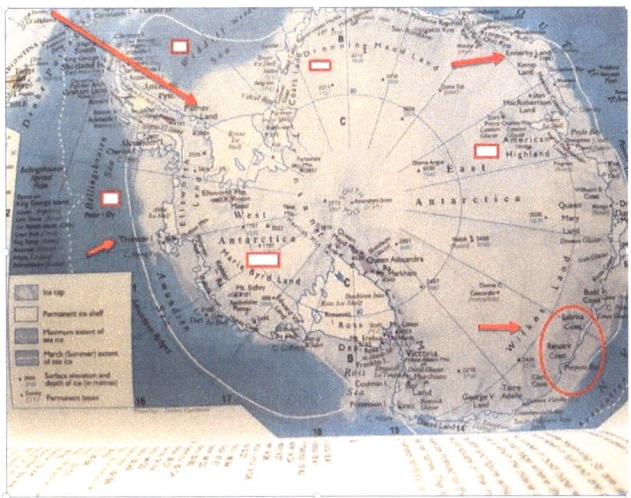

Sauhra is a wet place, in fact one of the wettest places on earth. Sauhra is also dry for four months of the year and unbearably cold for all 12 months of the year. The temperature at the foothills of Sauhra can touch minus 60 degrees Celsius above the ground. What is now known to exotic tourists as the Sauhran foothills are home to the albino penguin and the whale seal. The blood lagoon is around three hundred metres around the bend of the southern coast. It is a bleak coast with no distinguishing geological features except for a cliff and a deep fissure leading to a series of underground caves around 50 meters below the cliff.

35

The albino penguins are aggressive, necessarily so, since it is a carnivorous breed, and eats anything with blood and flesh on it. The animal can grow to a height of around 7 feet, is white, furry and has variously been mistaken for a polar bear or a bear of some species. The albino penguin lived on the frozen land ice. The whale seal was large but not overly aggressive. They are typically around forty to fifty feet in length, a mottle greying color. The whale seal lives to an approximate age of 60 years, and feeds on anything, absolutely anything that dwells in the water. This seal basks on land and can swim to depths of over 400 meters for hours at a stretch, hunting for kill. There are around 14,000 albino penguins at Sauhra, and around Sauhra there are an estimated 300 whale seals. The whale seals and albino penguins ignore each other, and over the millennium appear to have fed on everything else in the region. For two months of the year, the waters around Sauhra are visited by a few great whites, ambitiously hunting the whale seal. The water often turn bloody, sometimes with seal, sometimes with shark blood, sometimes with both. Whale seals are not known to submit meekly, however sloppy they may appear, and they have a massive grunt and roar, can flip over on the water with their entire body weight.

The Blood Lagoon, is so called because it is a massive, the largest, dumping ground for blood, medical waste, solar cell waste, carbon waste and nuclear waste on the planet. The Blood Lagoon is a pool that is around 4 kilometers deep, brimming with waste and bordered by a mountain of around 3,000 meters, piled with waste delivered by the waste tankers of various countries. The temperatures render the waste impotent and therefore environmentally safe, until picked up by starships for delivery to the junkyards of Mars. Most of these starships are unmanned, scoop, flight and deliver, one way flights, the craft itself being junked at the end of the journey on Mars. Space cadets called these starships Dominos, affectionately after the pizza delivery teams that crisscrossed the globe.

Rear Admiral Liui Eitenbolt (of Serbian origin) was cold, cold and worried. He stood on the deck swathed in warm uniformed clothing. Liui was Captain of the BNS Wen Heng, a Chinese battleship, especially built for the Antarctica.

The BNS Wen was massive and a very formidable ship. China's first large deep sea battleship could stay at sea for over four years without refueling, powered by nuclear engines. The ship had as many as thirty two decks and a crew of 6,700 personnel. The Wen could cut through ice, submerge totally if required to a depth of 1,500 meters and had a top speed in clear water of 22 knots. The Wen also carried formidable defense and armaments. 156 top end multi role fighter aircraft were based on the Wen with full nuclear strike capabilities. The ship had 14 field guns each of 200mm. Cruise missiles and anti-aircraft systems were all part of the armament on board. The BNS Wen had a compartmentalized super structure that could be detached and operated in segments at will, and was therefore virtually unsinkable. Personnel, geological, administration and medical used around 40 light aircraft and helicopters from the ship, on routine sorties and flights. The Wen had four separate landing strips on different levels that could be exposed or withdrawn as required. The infantry on board the Wen had numerous armored personnel carriers of the all-weather type, and a deck with over 70 battle tanks for invasive force when required. China had used the BNS Wen effectively off the East Coast of Africa to seize oil fields, off the West Coast of South America and in the South China Seas in victorious and highly successful battles at sea.

Liui was worried because of he had just been informed that unusual activity within a well-known group of whale seals was spotted off the northern coast of Sauhra. Whale seals usually experienced such active disturbance only during the great white season or when a super carrier or a nuclear submarine was headed into the waters. The whale seals could sense these disturbances even when they were around 4 days away so Liui figured he had some time on his hands to prepare for what was coming their way. 'Get Command brass into conference at 1400' Liui hoarsely texted his adjutant general. 'All of them? queried Sui Kin 'No, no, just the ones on shift, awake, on coffee' Liui ground out. At any point in time only around twenty percent of the senior brass on the

Wen were on active duty, not counting those on board on leave, geological research, development, combat exercises, Domino delivery program training and environmental studies. The Wen had on one of the largest libraries on board with over ten million volumes, both in hard back and paper back, together with a research facility that was all of over 400,000 square meters and fully equipped in ways that would put many laboratories to the sword of envy.

Sui Kin rattled off a chain of commands on his smart communicator and set matters in motion. The Smart Communicators were a relatively new piece of equipment delivered to the top brass of the BNS Wen. The communicators could stay in touch with any part of the planet and also during a fourteen hour window communicate with any manned or unmanned Dominos on Mars, or on the way to Mars.

1400 saw a sober Command brass trooping into conference. Liui looked at them, a majority were of South East Asian origin however, there were some Africans and even Indians among the top echelons. Command brass at 1400 had 28 senior officers, including a major general, two air marshals, several ship captains and four nuclear submarine commanders. BNS Wen was usually accompanied by a flotilla of destroyers, cruisers, four submarines and support ships. The Sheang Wok was the largest nuclear submarine, a full four hundred metres in length and at its widest 800 feet. The Sheang had the call sign Crispy because it virtually fried any object it targeted with its laser weapons that had a range of over 4,000 miles, with an accuracy of within four feet.

Capn Cook of the Crispy Sheang

Liui looked at the Crispy commander, ironically, call sign Capn Cook 'any advance information Cook'. 'Odds are it's a full carrier group with an attack nuclear submarine, Admiral' Cook replied looking at some notes, his cigar tapping ash out gently. 'Probably of North American origin Liui grimaced 'who else would throw in a carrier group at Sauhra with Domino launches due for end of the week'. Liui looked at Sui Kin who quickly put up the huge multi-dimensional hologram map of the region. 'Two divisions at American Highlands, one at Enderby Land. Command centre on the opposite side at Marie Byrd Land, depth one thousand metres.' Liui never went into a Command meeting without a plan 'Target the lane Palmer to Shetland to King George to Falkland Islands with BNS Wen cruise missiles – setting on radar detection. 'Sub bases at Weddell Sea and Bellingshausen Sea. 'What about Wen artillery' queried Captain Volokov.

'Negative' Liui smiled 'we will submerge the Wen at 1600 tomorrow to a depth of 1,000 metres off the sheltered side at Thurston Island. All aircraft on board to be moved to the Wilkes landing bay field'. 'All aircraft at Wilkes? Raised eyebrows from Air Marshal Weiner. Not one to let go, Liui quickly jumped in 'Alternatives, Marshal?

Weiner had at one point been top competition for Command head at the BNS Wen and still looked the part for most of it, except for his Socialist leanings, however, Weiner was an excellent military strategist. 'I would agree with leaving the bombers at Wilkes, but would put the multi-role fighters at Dronning Maud and leave the copters and most of the light aircraft sprinkled around the divisions for air and logistics support'. 'You do realize Marshal that you are preparing for an all-out attack formation, based essentially on disturbances among Sauhra whale seals? Liui frowned 'The mobilization cost will take off over a trillion from our training and maneuver projects over the next two years and we will probably have to push forward the nuclear renewals a bit'. Weiner grimaced 'The downside risk of not doing enough is to lose the launch platform to Mars, the Blood Lagoon and the access to mineral resources. Rare mineral deposits are too valuable to be left behind with the garbage'.

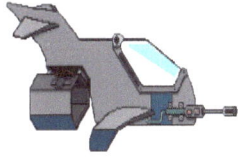

Three days later, the BNS Wen and accompanying forces had been redeployed. The Wen sat quietly at the bottom of the sea off Thurston Island, a foreboding silent, dark, glowing inverted structure, camouflaged entirely in an underwater ice parka that was sonar and radar resistant. On the fourth day, the carrier group arrived off King George. The carrier group was the Scarred Reefer carrier group. It included the formidable 180,000 tonne aircraft carrier with over 300 all-weather attack fighters, 11 destroyers or cruisers, four battleships and no less than 11 submarines.

They were clearly primed to take on anything that came their way. The Sheang Wok 'Crispy' sat still in the water, in full view, its conning tower a full fourteen stories high, waiting for instructions from Liui. International law needed the Crispy to be displayed in full view, except when in battle formation and Liui did not want a premature diplomatic incident. The sheer size and ability to evade detection, of the Crispy made it a danger to any sea going vessel, and it was therefore required to ride in the open unless in actual battle formation. The Crispy was actually originally designed as a ship to maneuver the ice lakes on Mars when the settlers reported that the lakes were too deep and too frozen to permit navigation with the usual ice road runners. The Crispy's second generation twin sister Deep Fry was now settled on the ice lakes of Mars, farming the vegetation hundreds of kilometers below the surface into the ice.

Liui Eitenbolt was a cautious man. He had tucked away his marine infantry divisions in three separate regions, likewise the submarines and the aircraft. The mighty Wen itself sat now quietly at the bottom off Thurston Island. Liui waited along with Volokov and Sui Kin in the command centre on the Wen, sipping coffee and forking noodles spiced with fresh lamb pieces. Sui Kin monitored communications and soon reported that Admiral McGuiness of the Scarred Reefer was on the line. McGuiness was an old sea hand with a sharp mind, very aggressive but farsighted at the same time. 'What's up, Lew'? McGuiness queried 'What's all the activity about, the formations and the signals in? Liui 'Whale seals and albinos off their course, Mac and too many of your ships in the area for this time of the year. No drills notified by your team and at least two Dominos are reported late, very late. The last time a Domino was late, was, well, never'. 'Dominos late? McGuiness sounded genuinely surprised 'Stay still, we will hold positions too and see what this is about'. Sui Kin stepped in 'We are now getting tracking information on the Wen radar showing an incoming aircraft, no spacecraft, no space fleet, a large one, heading for our position, arrival in seventeen hours'.

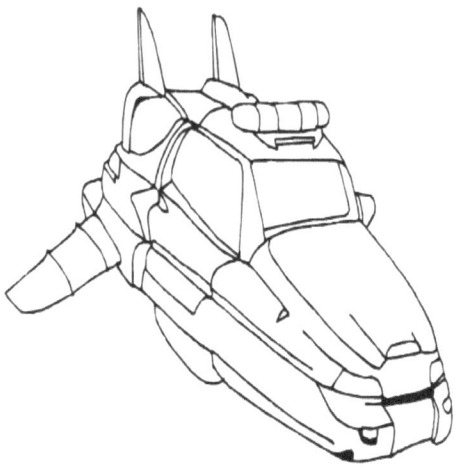

In a few hours, it was clear to both Liui and McGuiness that a massive alien space fleet was headed their way. Liui took the unusual step to go over to the Scarred Reefer to confer with McGuiness's team. It was Liui's first visit to the massive carrier. The 180,000 tonne aircraft carrier had two layered open to sea decks with over 300 all-weather attack fighters parked, 15 destroyers/ cruisers/ battleships in close cluster formation and no less than 11 submarines with their cones walking water around the carrier. It was a formidable sight over a ten kilometer radius, and clustered together like that they would have an impenetrable shield.

Within three hours, the Scarred Reefer received a communication, garbled at first, it contained no coherent message. It was repeated thrice and McGuiness was unable to respond as it simply could not be understood. Silence then for another four hours. Four hours since Sui Kin had received the first input on the Wen's systems. The next communication was in perfect English 'Hello, McGuiness'. 'Quite different from the expected 'greetings earthlings' conventionally expected' Liui remarked smiling. 'McGuiness, my goodness, that is quite a show of force, very unnecessary, I may assure you' the Voice continued 'we are merely here in response to an invite'. 'An invite?! McGuiness could not help himself, this was all going a bit too far 'invite, invade? Invite with a fleet of spaceships? And how many of you are there? 'Allow me to introduce myself, McGuiness' the Voice replied calmly 'I am in your terms a senior research assistant and we are around 200 visions'. 'Visions? McGuiness exclaimed. 'Yes, Visions as we have no physical form, we are here peacefully to attend the meeting of the inner earths'. 'Inner earth?? Both Liui and McGuiness looked at each other startled and puzzled.

 'Allow me to explain' the Voice went on 'by the way, how is my friend Captain Cook doing on the Crispy? (By now Liui and McGuiness had ceased being surprised at anything the Voice said). Your planet has a Sand inner earth, Volcano inner earth, Forest inner earth and Ocean inner earth. Four inner earth systems each interconnected with each other, each system around 12,000 of your meters below your surface area. All sands, volcanos forests and oceans are connected with each other and have their own colonies of inhabitants known to us for millions of years as the Medivians.' 'Inhabitants !?? Liui and McGuiness burst out involuntarily. 'The Medivians located on Earth around five million of your years previously, pardon any language inaccuracies, I am using one of your Scarred Reefer translators online, real time. The Medivians actually own the planet and tolerate your surface existence and intrusions. They were originally on Mars, as you may well have suspected or expected, and arrived here after the demise of their planet. We, I, am from Venus, we discarded physical forms a few

millennia ago for our current virtual visions. In two hours, we will be within your planet, you will not be disturbed, and our ships will hold their perimeter in your upper atmosphere. My name for your reference is SERA. We will leave in three earth days after the festivities'. 'Festivities!!? 'Yes, of course' Sera continued 'since we are here, we will observe the performances of our representatives at your Olympics'. 'Representatives!!?? Sera could almost be heard smiling 'Yes, we have all had along with the inner earth systems, representatives in all your fields from time to time, to see how competitive you were as a race. Athletics, racquet sports, track and field, team sports – you name it. At some point of time, we have had our representatives participating'. 'Did they win? Liui asked. 'Always' Sera replied, every occasion, every field, breaking your records. In science we used our representatives to introduce key events and what you then call discoveries'. 'But, you don't have physical forms, you are visions'. McGuiness countered.

'Oh, our representatives assume the life form of your people, each time a Vision is selected to be a representative. It is really, quite simple. We have even done it with horses and occasionally other animals. Every few years we take part in an inconclusive conflict, to test weapons. We are thankful for your people providing us these opportunities to test new sciences and weapons. How are some of my favourites doing? Federer, Ussain Bolt, Steffi Graf, Lance Armstrong, Ben

Johnson'. 'Lance and Johnson were doping cheats' McGuiness shot back. 'Yes, we had to do that, it was getting awkward, there was no logical way to explain their performances at the time' Sera replied sounding sad. 'Bradman, Laver and Federer pretty much got away though and we were pleased with that. Why, most of your Nobel laureates are either Visions or Medivians'. 'Anyway, what sort of a name is Sera' Liui queried do you have a cultural gene' 'No, we are missing that, Sera is simply short for senior research assistant' Sera sounded even more sad. 'Any words of advice? McGuiness put in. Sera replied 'Not really, but I will give you a list of some well-known Visions who have done time here. The list includes Alexander, Sitting Bull, Socrates, Aristotle, 132 religious leaders, Einstein, Newton, Aryabhatt, CV Ramakrishnan, Steve Spielberg, George Lucas, Humphrey Bogart, Henry Fonda, Bruce Willis, Van Damme, Schwarzenegger, Gregory Peck, Akbar, Chandragupta, Neil Armstrong (whom we almost took back), Jesse Owens, Phelps, and so many others' '132 religious leaders? Sui Kin interrupted 'of all or any religions? 'Yes, pretty much, those 132 includes 2 Dalai Lama, one Buddha and 23 popes among others. We had originally planned for Hitler to be a religious leader, however, he chose the military at a young age'. 'No Gandhi or Mandela in the list? 'No, Gandhi, Mandela and Mother Teresa were yours alone, earthlings, we learnt much from them. We learnt compassion, forgiveness and sacrifice from earthlings. Your unique values, values without recompense, strange concepts in this galaxy, in fact in the universe, I believe'. Liui was warming up to the whole concept 'Are the top five wealthy families also Visions or Medivians? 'No, never, wealth creation is a uniquely self-defeating, purposeless, human enterprise. You accumulate material things which you cannot transform into infinity, into values or universal systems. You can only create joy, peace through your instruments of compassion, forgiveness and sacrifice, not from dust. Your craze for gold dust and others is frankly both amusing and sad.

You lose yourself in the dust of sands. Even the Sand Medivians do not so lose themselves. You have some intelligence, yourself, Sui. I invite you to lose form and become a Vision. You can then return as you wish, take any form, be an elephant or an ant or even a politician' Sera burst out laughing'. 'Sui a politician? Not likely' Liui mused 'But he could yet be a monk or a famous Aladdin (he has a lamp in his cabin) or a black golfer, a black tennis star or a yellow basketball star. I have to get myself one of these Medivian beings as part of my trophy collection on the Wen'. 'That's just it' Sera sadly remarked 'Humans think of everything as a part of a collection, an accumulation, even art, artifacts, you cheapen value through accumulation, everything has to be bigger, brighter, faster, stronger with you. The strength of the weakness you do not feel, the poor always inherit, long after the kings turn to dust'. 'Why haven't we caught you on radar before? McGuiness said

'Is this your first trip in a while? Sera laughed 'No, we make frequent trips in fact, however, we usually park on the far side of the moon, where we are unseen. Solar flares this time around forced us to come in more directly. We did not want to alarm you, so alerted the whale seals in advance. Sometimes we land directly in the desert in Texas, always using the homing beacons as a faithful guide'. 'Homing beacon? Liui jumped in 'You have a homing beacon here on earth? 'Of course, else we would never make it so accurately this far, what else did you think Stonehenge, the Inca Sun Temple, and the Sphinx pyramids are?

'If you are so advanced, why at all do you come to Earth? Liui challenged 'and why do you need the beacons? Sera (sounded serious, McGuiness later remarked) quickly replied 'Earth and all of you humans are our entertainment. You are nothing more than a reality show for us, a toy, a great puzzle, a strategy and pieces on a chess board. Very interesting and at times very repetitive. In the past, several times, we have swept all of the pieces off the board and started anew, a new game, a new species….very amusing. Floods, tornadoes, hurricanes, droughts, climate change are all variable keys in the game'. McGuiness could almost hear Sera grinning.

Nine Tales

It was getting late enough to be worried. I once again stepped into the balcony and looked down. Except for a drenched street dog that was lying down miserably near the gate, there was not a soul to be seen anywhere. Rain water had puddled under the lamp post. A breeze ruffled the mango tree in the courtyard and a few twigs fell down and broke. Thunder rumbled in the distance. Did I hear a soft knock at the door? I turned back and headed for the door. It was the milkman and my mom opened the door and took the customary large measures of milk from his aluminum can. How he managed to get around in this weather mystified me. It was morning, and yet the sky was overcast and dark, punctured by bursts of lightning and thunder. I wondered if my favorite tree would survive the onslaught. Last monsoon we lost a large tree, it had some sort of berries, and everybody complained about the carpet of sticky, gooey berries beneath the tree.

Milk on the boil, mom in the kitchen, it was time for me to get some serious relaxation time clocked. I curled up on the sofa, pushing my head into the cushion, legs hooked under me. The television was on but only static, the rain must have knocked out the cable or satellite dish as it usually did. I lived alone with Mom after Dad left us. He walked out one day in his military uniform and I never saw him return. For a long time, Mom was sad and cried, mostly quietly. Ladies came and sat with her, but it was really a gossip, not a comfort circle. The children, Mickey and Juggy were long gone. One packed his bags and went off to some other country and Juggy (I think) joined the military like his father. He dropped in briefly once a year to see Mom, usually during the festival of lights and fireworks.

The milkman was a strange one. He wrapped a large cloth (which at some time had been a bluish white) around his head. He seemed to actually enjoy lugging around the heavy aluminum can each morning, and then cycling off. The other regular visitor was a doctor of sorts. I never understood what he really did for Mom. I think he was what they called a quack. He had these small bottles of even smaller pills and colorful liquids, some to be sipped, some oils. We used to have postman deliveries but that died out and Mom seemed to have to walk down to the post office to collect her mail. Our village was small, we were short at various times of a barber, plumber, postman and even a village idiot. That last was soon rectified when we got the new sarpanch.

Mom had visited the big city Delhi. On her way back to her sister's house, she saw me by the road side, thin, forlorn looking. Mom took me by the hand and had something to eat arranged for me. She did look around enquiring for my parents, but that turned out to be a dead end. So, to my delight, Mom wrapped me up and took me home, just like that. It's been 15 or more good years since. Well, how could I leave out a little detail? I died around 4 years back.

The milkman had come to deliver the morning milk. I rushed out as usual, giving him a friendly rub around his bare legs. He was carrying the large milk aluminum can. He usually dropped off a spoons of milk on the slab at the side which cats always appreciate. But, this time he tripped. I don't think it was my fault. He seemed to trip on the stairs. The aluminum can fell on me. The milk was all over the place, the can broke my back and nearly cut my body in half. I think I died within half a minute, a painful thirty seconds. Mom came rushing out screaming, but there was nothing she could do. The milkman was wailing something awful. He dug a deep hole near the largest tree in the garden. Mom wrapped me in my favorite towel, then put me a large shoe box, and lowered me gently in to the hole. The milkman slowly piled on the earth over the box and all that remained was a little mound of earth near the tree.

It was night when I woke up. I could surprisingly move my legs and there was no pain. I pushed upward and seemed to simply move lightly through the box and the earth over it. Soon I was standing outside the door, feeling a little foolish. I clambered over a window plant and walked into Mom's room, climbed onto the bed and cuddled up against her. She did not seem to notice. I let her sleep. After a while, I got up and walked away. I had left no mark on the bedspread, there were no telltale paw prints, I was in fact quite dead. I walked out to the steps at the front door where I had died less than 24 hours earlier. That was when I got a shock.

Dad was sitting on the steps looking a bit lost and low. I climbed onto his lap and he absently stroked me gently. I asked him 'Chief, what are you doing here? 'Oh, pussy, I've been here for years, the light did not come for me. I was a sniper with the 4th infantry and my last shoot was a doctor having his coffee in a tent around two hundred meters away. Good shot, took the fuel tank near the tent square in the centre, the tent went up in the blast – no tent, no doctor. Guess, I have not been forgiven that one yet'. I did not know what to say, I was quite new to all of this anyway. 'Does Mom know you're here? I asked softly. 'She can't see me' Lt. Dilbaug Yadav said, a large tear drifting down one cheek aimlessly, till it lost itself in my fur. 'Well, you're not alone now, you've got me till the light comes for you' I tried to comfort him. I got back into the house and sprawled out on the sofa. Idly waiting for the morning. I would give that dog under the tree the fright of his life one of these days.

Time went on. Nobody noticed my presence. It's as if I just did not exist. Except for one clever family. Like all houses in the village we had rats. Small rats, big rats, medium sized rats. Somehow the little fellows sensed me but could not see me. They were scared of the danger and simply vanished. Mom was of course delighted and the neighbors wondered why we did not have rats and the ever present wall lizards. They put it down to all the time Mom had on her hands to keep her home clean. I did not want nine lives. I was quite happy with Mom and did not seriously think there was a bright light coming for me anytime soon. I had mercilessly killed too many rats.

The Wrong 'Un

The rain splattered on the asbestos shutter. It was dark. Still summer, but an early shower. Kedar looked out the kitchen window. It was early, four in the morning but he was wide awake. His tea was on the boil, the aroma of the tea leaves wafting up slowly. The events of the past few days had surprised him, made him think of the possibilities. As a fifteen year old there were a lot of possibilities, he supposed. His neighbor and best friend was a fourteen year old submissive, tag along, by the name of Sridhar. Sridhar played a bit of cricket occasionally in the small ground at the back of the row of houses. Sometimes he even bowled at the wall himself when he had nobody to play with. He never did strike Kedar as particularly talented but enjoyed the game, never fussed over injury, never tried to cheat as most of his teammates often did. Sridhar often spent time chasing the ball, fielding, and did not often get an opportunity to bat or bowl. When asked he did so, but was never very successful with the bat, too careful, probably. Still, at fourteen years of age, there were bound to be possibilities. Fitness? Well, they were all fit at that age...it was that age.

 Much of that had changed last week. Their school Davidson High School [DHS], was taking part in the high school seniors, inter school cricket tournament, the Hornby Hooles Shield. Hornby was a governor or sheriff about a hundred years back. Kedar sipped his tea. Nobody even knew who Hornby was, but the tournament was funded and held every year, end of summer, by some trustees. A tournament held by eighty year olds for fifteen year olds. Davidson had a good team. Five good batsmen, a decent not too nervous wicketkeeper and five steady bowlers who landed the cherry generally in decent length and around the stumps. The team had reached the semi-finals twice and the finals once in the past five years. So they were noted as a good team with a good coach.

Davidson had a school bus that took the team for their matches. Davidson also had Muthu as their coach. Muthu was a sports coordinator and helped the cricket team and the badminton team prepare. He was a good reader of the mind game and had a reputation of knowing just how to prepare the team for the games. Everybody liked Muthu, and Muthu liked cricket, badminton and grooming the boys. He was not a serious, strict coach. He genuinely liked the sports and training the boys. He seemed to have endless patience and concentration. The school bus was a diesel, 4 litre stretched van chassis that carried 15 to 20 students at a squeeze. The bus had been painted blue and white a few years back and had the school name and shield painted on both sides for good measure or pride or both. This was India. School bus, vans were just about any old color, not yellow and black, even taxis were no longer yellow and black in Mumbai but equine blue. Currency notes were green, blue, orange, brown and even purple in India.

That Sunday, the bus carried fourteen, the twelve team members, coach Muthu and an assistant. There was also a pile of equipment piled at the back of the van. The school bus swerved to avoid a stray dog, a mongrel ambling across the road. A mangy, dripping, patchy, black and white lean mongrel. A nothing dog. But, thought Kedar, a dog who did his job. The van braked, turned on its right front wheel, swung around and went into a skid. It slammed into the building on the right of the street, a concrete pillar front, for car parking, gates and entrance. Six students suffered bruises and cuts, four had fractures of the arm or legs. Muthu and the bus driver were shaken but alright. The team was short now four players for a match two hours away. Muthu called the Principal, made sure that the injured boys were rushed to the nearest hospital for x-rays and treatment. Parents were informed. Police and insurance reports were duly filed, the driver questioned for hours. Late evening, Muthu was back at the school gym. The school's first match was forfeit. They were four players short and starting the tournament tomorrow at the bottom of the table. Each team had 15 overs to bat and bowl. Each bowler could bowl only a maximum of three overs. They simply could not play with 6 bruised students. Frantic calls were made to teachers in other classes, to parents of the team members. Five replacements were eventually decided upon late night past eleven. Sridhar was one of them, somebody casually having mentioned his name as a player who did a bit of both, batting and bowling.

First match out on Monday. A somber DHS team took the field, won the toss, and chose to bat. Sridhar was sent out to open, he was considered weak and if he lost his wicket early, it would be no big loss for the side. At home, Sridhar was a quiet batsman, the reason being that a lofted shot could break a window pane. The last time this happened, he received ten swishes with the cane and no pocket money for two weeks. After a few quiet shots, Sridhar realized that no window panes would break here on an open ground. He was free. He opened his young shoulders. Lofting, pulling, sweeping high, smashing through the covers. At the end of fifteen overs, Sridhar returned having faced 62 balls and scored 124 runs. DHS had scored a huge total of 197 runs in 15 overs. Their opponents Sunrise HS were shaken but determined. They put shoulder to wheel, to the task and were soon 135 for 4, with an even chance of winning the match back. Good careful batting.

At 135 for 4 the bruised skipper, on a chance decided to give Sridhar the ball. Sridhar bowled slow left arm around the wicket. Floating the ball in from the edge of the crease and gently turning it away from the right hander on or around the off. Only ever so often the ball did not turn away but came in straight through. Sridhar ended up with 4 wickets for 12 runs and DHS were home dry. In the next two matches a quiet Sridhar continued to score heavily. In addition to the slow, around the wicket left arms, he could also apparently bowl equally well, right arm around the wicket. Same trick but in reverse. Stock ball turns into the right hander and the odd one straightens out or moves away. Six matches later, DHS were Harris Hooles Shield winners for the first time. The school was talking about college and private company interest in the find of the year, the amazing Sridhar.

Kedar grimaced. Strong, but still it was good tea. He was fifteen. He had done everything he could possibly could at the age of fifteen to get into the school cricket team. It had taken a lot of timing to let the dog out of the gate at exactly the right time as the van headlights rounded the bend in the street, but the mongrel had done his job. He knew that Sri the driver had a soft spot for dogs, strays. Sridhar's unexpected call up and rise to fame would make like more difficult for him, more pressure from his parents. Everyday sucking up Sridhar's new fame. The silly boy really seemed to have a talent for the game, at least for now. Kedar drained off the last tea. Well, he had to go. Muthu was also badminton coach and time to get into badminton practice. Dear Muthu could at least be counted on to get him into the badminton team. Otherwise accidents to coaches did happen and maybe a new coach was not such a bad idea after all.

The Far West in Africa

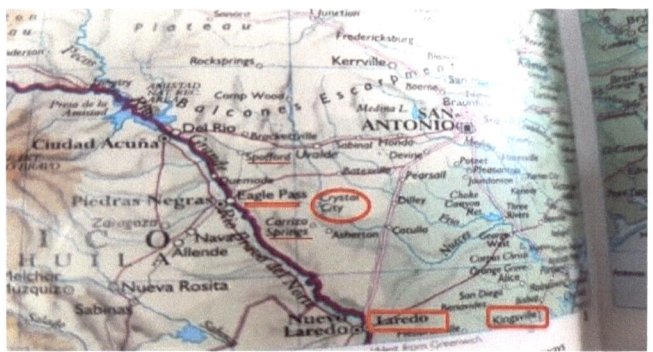

Wallis was known as JW. He was young, twenty four and at that age, one did things without necessarily thinking it through fully. Wallis was born in the high dry mountains of Eagle Pass off the Rio Grande on the border of Mexico. Eagle Pass was close to Crystal City and then San Antonio. Untamed mustangs, miles without water, rattle snakes, Mexican bandits, Texan outlaws, were all par for the course. JW looked after his colts. He was not a fast draw artist but accurate and had that rare quality of a gunman at twenty four – courage in the face of fire He was slick with a colt .45 slung from the hip, slung low but not too low. JW was also equally good with both hands so carried a colt at each hip. This was an advantage, a huge advantage, although he was far more accurate and steady with the right hand. JW also could rapid fire his right hand colt by fanning the hammer of the revolver with the thick leather gloved palm of his left hand.

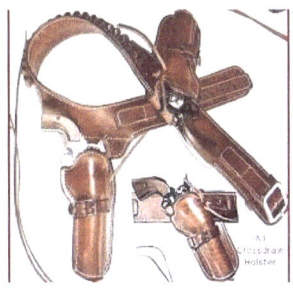

The two single action revolvers were an investment by JW. Wallis knew that to stay alive and productive where he was, he needed the best firearm by his side. He used the colt frontier six shooter, first made in 1877. While it had all of the advantages which came with the reliable colt, the big advantage was that it took the .44 Winchester cartridges. A Winchester was an invaluable sidekick when in the mountains. Wallis was good with a Winchester, really good at 100 meters within two feet. JW used a yellow boy 1866 Winchester and could trim the whiskers off a wolf at that distance. Wallis stacked a pile off a group of Mexican bandidos who happened to dearly depart and leave behind, horses, rifles, stores and some gold.

He wanted more. That was when, sitting in a bar at Carrizo Springs, Wallis was a bit surprised to see two tall, heavy set, African looking men. The alcohol clearly was far too easy for them. Wallis joined them out of curiosity and lo and behold they did speak a smattering of American. The story that he got was that somewhere at Quemado, a ways off from Carrizo but closer to Eagle Pass, was an African elder with a map to an ancient gold mine in East Africa. One of Solomon's mines, a river of gold.

Quemado did have the African and he told his story to anybody willing to listen. He was not partial and only needed the assurance of two bottles of the finest powerful local whiskey. Wallis decided to outfit and after a short coach ride (he hated horseback riding unless unavoidable) to nearby Spoford decided to outfit at Spoford. A large double edged blade, couple of water canteens, blankets, several boxes of cartridges and some dry sticks of dynamite, JW headed out south. He stopped by Fort Laredo, then went on to Kingsville before going through Bishop to Corpus Christi. He was glad that he had stored up at Spoford, everything seemed twice as expensive at Corpus Christi. At Corpus Christi, there was no ship to Africa. JW had to go further east to Port Lavaco off Matagorda and the Palacios to find a ship to Africa, East Africa. Port Lavaco was a wild place at the time and probably still is. It took JW two gunfights in which he put down one gent and winged four more, before trouble avoided him.

Months of a gut wrenching sea journey later, Wallis was stopped off West Africa at Pointe Noire, Cabinda. From there he wrangled a berth to Cape Town, changing two ships along the way. Wallis spent a further month taking time off at Cape Town before he could ship out to Durban, Maputo before stopping off at Beira. Beira was thickly forested at the time, and probably is not now. Beira was off jungle and looked threatening. Wallis had further up East Africa to go. Here the boats looked less sea worthy and more shark worthy. Seventy foot trawlers littered with fish were seemingly the most luxurious accommodation from there. His trawler hugged the coast line and cut across only to head for Mahajanga on the coast of Madagascar. After an onward stop for provisions at Mayotte Mamoudzou and west to Maroni, JW finally reached Delgado in lower Malawi.

Delgado proved to be a dead end, off the leather painted map that JW carried. He realized that he needed to move further down. At Quissanga on the coast, at a dusty, thatched open bar, Wallis met two British traders. Harvey and Tanery. Harvey offered to fine tune JW's map for him, JW not revealing his final destination of his purpose. Tanery spent most of his time in drunken stupor waiting for the next ship of supplies to stock up. H&T Trading bought off ships, and sold locally tackle, canned food, ammunition, rawhide rope, canvas, some weapons thought not often, and lots of alcohol which was their premium stock item. JW took a boat eventually from Quissanga south to an inlet called Memba. He was running out of gold and tradeable items now, having had to do a number of deals to get this far.

From Memba, Wallis took two donkeys, a bags of crushed maize, beans, biscuit, bacon and dried beef jerky. Each donkey carried a Winchester (JW had bought another one off Harvey) and one of the donkeys carried a drum of cartridges and a shotgun with a bag of cartridges. The shotgun also bought at H&T Trading was an unplanned opportunistic buy. A left over at H&T, it had a good action, an 1887 Browning repeating sawn off shotgun. Wallis himself rode a compliant mule, compliant but independent when it came to snacking off shrubs. Other than that, it was a relatively quiet ride through rolling shrub land, sparsely littered with thickets and largish trees every 100 meters or so. Wallis arrived at the huckle hick town of Namapa.

Namapa had four buildings and a stable. Wallis was not sure which looked more hospitable, and decided to eat his beans and maize, drink cheap whisky, later sleeping in the stable hay not far from his supplies, mule and donkeys. At the Namapa inn, Wallis for the first time since he left America heard some talk of the fabled rivers and mine of gold. He was a little worried that it was not such a big secret and was quite well known in local lore. Anything so well-known was unlikely to have retained its pristine glory or wealth. Had he come a long way for nothing? His leather map showed him that he had nearly two hundred miles to go, across the Lurio. The Lurio was a scenic, quiet river, crossable at several shallow points. The water was clear blue and Wallis drank upstream while the mule and the donkeys watered themselves up downstream. Small luxuries. North of the Lurio was Montepuez, a town larger than Namapa. Montepuez had even a pastor, a sheriff, a doctor and a small hotel in addition to a place of worship, the jail house and four or five trading buildings. There were a lot of Africans about and half a dozen or so westerners around. For the first time Wallis even saw horses, which he later learnt were left overs of a column of soldiers once stationed there by the French. Wallis was even more dismayed when he learnt at the not so grand Grand Melangois Hotel, that French soldiers had been posted to the mine, Solomon's mine.

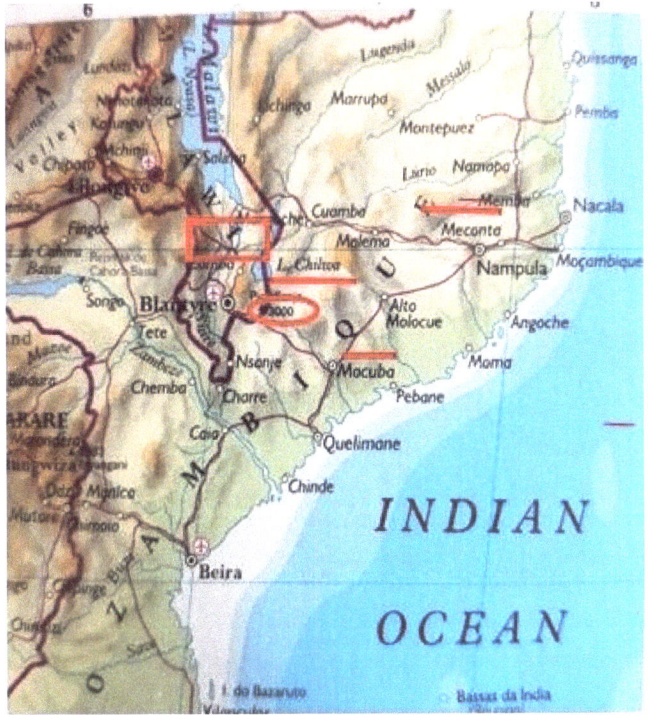

Not wanting to walk into any former soldiers, Wallis moved on after a day and a half at Montepuez. Soldiers here did not desert, they simply stayed back. Now closely following the corrections in scratches made to his leather map made by Harvey at Quissanga, Wallis crossed the Messalo up north, then headed south to Marrupa. He came close once to blowing off the head of a large, very large and aggressive crocodile, and on another occasion almost used the shotgun on an ugly snake looking poisonous enough for a hundred mules. The mine, Solomon's was off Marrupa, clearly marked on his precious map taken from the African at Quemado off Spoford.

Wallis arrived at the marked outcrop of rocks around noon. Staying well back, he took out a long, folding looking glass, something else he had picked up at H&T and examined the land ahead. His position was just behind a high ledge that looked down over a stream and across the stream was a cave entrance. Not really a cave, it was a well carved out opening in the face of the hill opposite. The opening clearly led deeper into the hill. Wallis was dismayed. Everywhere there were discarded shovels, barrows, narrow gauge iron loader track leading into the hill, a small discarded shack and empty crates. This was no secret mine, it was a mine that was well worked. The minus was that for hundreds of years, maybe even thousands, the mine had been worked. On the plus side, this could also mean the wild stories of the river, streams and hill of gold were true.

There was a soft click behind him. The thing about trained mules and donkeys is that the spirit is completely taken out of them. They did not warn him of the approaching mule and its threatening rider. Wallis turned around slowly, lowering the long glass. About thirty feet away was a large (were there really any other kind in Africa) fat, burdensome to the mule, white man, raw pink in the face, closely cut hair and a thick brown beard. Wallis at the time, thought irrelevantly that the brown beard rather complimented the raw pink of the face. 'Logan' the stranger introduced himself. He had a rifle across the back of the mule, pointed idly down, in the direction of Wallis. 'Wallis' he countered 'here as a tourist, from San Antonio'. 'And where might that be? queried Logan, the rifle not shifting direction. This was not going well, and while Logan did not look threatening, he was definitely not a welcoming committee.

 Wallis was not tall, possibly around five seven, but lean. The long travel had made him leaner. He was not square jawed like many Texans from south west of Austin. He looked he had a shade of Mexican in him, just a shade though. He was now lying on his back on the rock, shelf edge, facing Logan on his mule. What happened next was smooth, not particularly fast, but Logan was clearly unprepared. Wallis rolled on his hip to his right, closer to a small boulder, at the same time, his left hand slapped leather and came up with the colt at this hip. Before he completed the roll, he snapped off a shot. The slug took Logan high in his left shoulder. Give the man credit. He did not go down. Within seconds he brought up the rifle and let loose. The first shot hit the dirt in front of Wallis and the second clipped the boulder. Wallis was not behind the boulder and Logan was still sitting on his mule, blood streaming from a hole in his shoulder. A stalemate then? Wallis had both his colts and two belts of cartridges, all the loops full. Wallis did not need two mules, he decided. From his position, he was well covered from Logan, and had a clear line of fire on his own mules and donkeys.

Wallis shot his mule bringing it down in a squealing, kicking slump, the two donkeys breaking into kicking and braying. Logan shifted in his seat and swing around. Wallis rolled away from the boulder and fired thrice before Logan fully realized what had happened. All three shots took Logan in the chest, this time, he fell over on the right, the rifle falling over the side of his mule. Chaos all around, Wallis was comfortable. Logan's mule joined the braying and kicking, Wallis' mule was still kicking around and his donkeys braying loudly. A few minutes, and two shots later from his colt, Logan and the downed mule were quiet.

Wallis took stock. He had Logan's mule, his rifle, a few more shells for the rifle, his two supply donkeys, and his supplies were intact. Taking the mule and donkeys down the slope he unburdened them, put them into the roughly hewn corral where there was some water and grass. Wallis decided to inspect Marrupa's famous mine or river of gold or hill of gold. The mine was unlike any other mine. While a single rail trailed off into the darkness, there were no obvious signs of excavation or digging. Maybe, thought Wallis, the gold was just there to be removed? Hundreds of years back. Wallis spent a couple of days around the mine, even panning the water at the stream nearby, but there was no trace of gold dust.

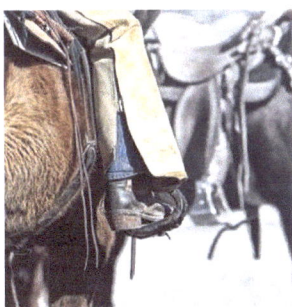 The mules looked restless, and while there was water, the grass and little hay was almost gone. The ground around was hard, rocky, dusty, boulder strewn, with some shrubs and the very

occasional tree. Wallis decided to trace back Logan, he could not have come from nowhere. It took Wallis an hour to find Logan's wooden shack near a tree. Logan was a self-styled lawman in the area. His shack had coffee, hard biscuits, some awful looking meat jerky, matches, two spare blankets, two tins of shells for his rifle and various assorted pots and pans. The shack had a bed, a table, two chairs and a side board of sorts. One window framed the wall facing he direction of the mine.

Wallis was practical. He had already concluded that there was no treasure at the Marrupa mine but remained confident that Africa would yield to him. He took the coffee, matches, blankets, two pots and a plate, leaving behind the biscuits which truth be told looked awful and probably tasted worse. His plan was to head back south, cross the Messalo again. From there on to Montepuez, across the Lurio and back to Memba for a ship all the way back to Freeport or Port Lavaco at Matagorda. Nearer the Messalo, there was a patch of a few hundred meters of more greenery, thick shrubs, closely set trees. Wallis was surprised as the African stepped out. He was tall, sparsely clothed, carried a spear as tall as him if not a few inches taller. The spear was wooden but steel tipped. Then, out behind the African stepped eleven more warriors. Warriors they were clearly were, painted all over their bodies in red and white markings and drawings, the faces mostly whitened out. All of them carried spears and some had long knives tucked through their waist bands. 'Cuamba' the African said loudly, by way of a sort of introduction, pointing his spear directly at Wallis. Wallis was still around 60 feet away from the group. But he was exposed with no cover around. He sat on his mule, his donkeys trailing behind, a peaceful but latent scene. He dismounted, took the reins of the mule in his right hand and walked toward the Africans. Cuamba and his eleven painted warriors were bunched together in a sort of reverse pyramid, front to back with three warriors including Cuamba in the front row and five or six at the back.

Wallis continued to walk forward and Cuamba became clearly increasingly agitated. He gestured downward with the point of his spear, clearly wanting Wallis to surrender in some form or action. When Wallis was about twenty five feet from them, he stopped. The mule walked ahead for two more steps. Wallis' right hand grabbed the shotgun on the left hip of the mule and came up firing. . The mule swerved right and trotted away. At twenty five feet, the shotgun fired into the middle of the group was devastating. Hot pellets peppered the group as Wallis got off three quick blasts. While two warriors fell to the ground, the others were shouting and running off in different directions, some trying to duck the hail of lead. Wallis dropped the shotgun and came up with both colt pistols, getting off shots to the left and right of the group.

Four warriors were on the ground, the rest had disappeared back into the trees. A spear thrown at him had creased his shoulder and another spear had landed point down in the sand in front of one of the donkeys. Grouping the mule and donkeys together, Wallis reloaded his colts not leaving a spare chamber, and checked that all the loops on his belt were full. He was well armed now. The two colts, the two rifles, one bought from H&T, the shotgun from H&T and Logan's Henry repeating rifle. For good measure, Wallis took one of the better looking long scythes from one of the fallen warriors, the spears being quite useless to him.

Wallis did not want to get into the trees where the remaining warriors had better cover. He had to go around. So he started walking parallel to the tree line with the mule and the donkeys. After around two hundred meters, he came to a ledge on the dry ground. The ledge led to a slope down to a stream. Across the stream was flat land and a way around. No cover anywhere around should the warriors want to try their hand again. He started down the slope and reached the stream without event. The stream was clearly a run off of the Messalo, and if he got across he could possibly still find a trail to Montepuez. A tranquil scene as he allowed the animals to water downstream and settled down further upstream.

Wallis heard the slight slithering, rustling, rattle behind him. He turned around slowly to see a thin, long yellowish snake, flat, poisonous, unfriendly head all reared up not more than ten feet behind him. Wallis was down on his haunches. He stood up slowly and took a step back, the snake swaying very gently before him. Instinctively, his right hand slapped the colt and came up firing. The first bullet nicked the rock behind the snake and the second was lucky, taking it a few inches below the head. It flipped over, not quite dead and Wallis had to put in a third bullet at close range to finish it. The three shots would have doubtless given his location away. Wallis looked around. The mule and donkey, were looking enquiringly at him, by now quite used to his gunplay and then resumed drinking. Further up, along the bank on his side, there was another ridge with a boulder, and sitting quietly along the ridge was a big cat and two cubs. It looked like some kind of leopard and the cubs must have been only a few months old. The cat stared unblinkingly at the scene below and

Wallis realized that it must have been watching him for a while. Doubtless the leopard was more interested in the animals, but wary of the weaponry recently demonstrated.

Wallis pitched camp. He needed to rest. After searching around, he collected enough dry sticks for a small fire, made some coffee and a meal of sorts with the old jerky and maize. The morning stretched lazily in front of him. He had not been disturbed at night and the leopard seemed to have moved on. Any attack would have caused a fearful kicking and braying from the animals. He crossed the ridge and headed on a path which would take him to around Montepuez. Straight ahead of him was a cluster of boulders and another extension of the tree line about a hundred meters to the left. There was some slight movement at the boulders. Mama leopard, papa leopard and the two cubs watched them from the boulders. Wallis stopped.

The cluster of boulders also had a water source as there was thick undergrowth and moss at one end. Then Cuamba made his appearance. If he looked warrior like before, he looked formidable, and very angry now. He was backed by more warriors, much more than Wallis would have like to see, nearly thirty or forty, a bunch of painted, angry, spear wielding warriors. Wallis stopped and dismounted. His mule and donkeys stopped, looking at him enquiringly. They wanted the water but sensed the leopard. The leopard wanted the animals but had not forgotten the gunplay. Cuamba had forgotten nothing, and was aiming to settle scores.

Wallis was tired, tired of this wild, unyielding place. He had nothing but trouble once at Marrupa. He stepped behind the mule and donkey, placing them between himself and the warriors and continued toward the boulders. Cuamba was still out of spear range. Wallis reached within thirty feet of the boulders, pulled the Winchester and let off three quick shots high onto the rocks. Cuamba stopped in his tracks, the shots ricocheting and whining around the boulders, pinging other rocks. The leopard family leapt warily away from the boulders, away from Wallis and Cuamba. The two cubs scrambling after, the mother half turning and looking back, patient still, knowing better things were to come. The leopards half walked, half sprinted to a clump of bushes less than fifty meters away and settled down to wait.

Wallis reached the boulders, unloaded the animals and took them away out of sight, behind a nook, still with access to water if they needed. He placed the shotgun, Henry, and two Winchesters around his small protection, with small handful piles of ammunition spaced out within his cover. He had about a hundred rounds for the rifles, twenty cartridges for the shotgun and around 50 bullets for the colts, not counting the twelve in the cylinders. Cuamba had closer to forty warriors. He raised his hand, palm facing upwards, dropped his spear and walked forward to Wallis.

Cuamba was accompanied by another warrior, whom he introduced as Luiga. Like Cuamba, Luiga did not carry his spear. 'That's far enough' Wallis called, when they were thirty feet away. Cuamba smiled 'You take your donkeys, food and leave, we will take your guns, coffee and blanket. Montepuez is not far from here, we will show you. From Montepuez, soldiers will take you to Namapa and then Memba.'

Wallis, it turns out had more than just a shade of Mexican bandido in him. He rifle shot Cuamba in the chest, and snapped off two more quick shots taking Luiga in the shoulder and then lower down in the stomach. The line of warriors behind them broke and spread out. Wallis dropped the Henry, grabbed the shotgun and let off two blasts. Cuamba and Luiga rushed forward spurting blood and grabbing at air. The next hour saw spears thrown in his direction. Five or six landing around him, clanging off the boulders and a few before him. With his rifles, he was regularly picking off warriors but he was running low on cartridges and not hitting enough. They were either lying low, hugging the terrain or suddenly rushing forward at angles.

The spear leaders, as Wallis called them would have been lethal, if they had a few bows and arrows or even a few rifles. He looked back and saw the leopard family watching the bloodletting calmly, patiently. Wallis was tired and the warriors sensed this. There were enough of them and he knew he did not have enough bullets. A group of determined warriors, spears and long knives in hand, started forward, spread out in a line, to his left. Wallis stepped up and out from behind the boulders, Winchester in right hand and shotgun in left hand. As he got within range, he left go first with the repeating Winchester and then when closer with the shotgun. He was not sure of what he hit or how many. He was just mad enough to throw everything he had at them. Standing, walking forward he fired until the shotgun clicked empty, seconds later the Winchester too. Carnage before him but several warriors with spears were still standing around, maybe ten. Wallis' grabbed a colt with his right hand and came up firing, fanning the hammer, then dropped the colt and started off with the left hand, emptying all six chambers in quick time. Standing before him were three warriors, one was a female, all crouched with spears held forward.

He turned and ran back toward the boulders, both colts, shotgun and rifle empty, dropped into the sand. Not cowardly, but Wallis had good survival instincts, he knew the value of a strategic retreat.

Sensing victory finally, the three ran after him. Closer to the boulders, he dived and grabbed Cuamba's spear, rolling on his side and throwing it forward. Not much time to aim, but the range was close. His spear throw took, the warrior in the centre, the female, through the right shoulder and she dropped to her knees with a soundless half scream, half hiss. The other two, long knives in hand, halted, and then rushed forward. The break in their stride gave Wallis time to scramble back, crawl leap over the boulders and grab the Henry. Almost immediately, the two warriors were over the boulders in much easier leaps. Wallis wielded the Henry like a club and tried to fend off their slashing knives. Both warriors were half crouched, one to his left and one to his right. Wallis had his Henry pointing butt forward toward them. He leapt back in a jump, his back smashing against the boulder, flipping the rifle stock backward at the same time. His back hit the boulder, with the stock of the Henry under his right arm and the rifle pointing toward the warriors. Immediately letting off three quick shots, taking one warrior in the thigh with his first shot and the other twice in the chest and stomach. It was all over in a few seconds.

Wallis took a deep breath, his back hurt terribly. He headed back toward the water source and dropped to his knees. The water was mossy but cool, a small trickle from nowhere fed the little pool. The mule and donkey were undisturbed in their sheltered nook. He recovered his colts, the action of the Winchester he had dropped was useless. He took the Henry and the remaining Winchester. He had just about six cartridges each for both and fed shells into the cylinders of both colts. Other than the around fifteen loops around his waist belt, he had no more cartridges for the colts. That was twelve, and fifteen a total of twenty seven bullets for the two colts. Looking around he found the shotgun but had only three shells remaining for the shotgun which he loaded and put onto the mule along with the two rifles.

Montepuez was not far and within the hour Wallis could see the smoke of little houses and buildings. He rode the mule into town and stopped at the first inn Le Pondemour. It was morning, and a heavy breakfast of mash potato, sausage, thick slices of bread liberally buttered, and curried beans was washed down by Wallis with a strong coffee. The Le Pondemour had a room available, his mule and donkeys were watered, fed and stabled. The room was around twenty by twenty feet with a small balcony overlooking the street. It had a bed with a thick mattress, all of seven by five feet, a wooden table, rocking and seating chairs and a cupboard. The facilities were a room leading from the main room, with exclusive use by the room's occupant. Wallis slept well, only once coming up in sweat with a dream about him going back to Eagle Pass at the Rio with no gold after his year of African adventure. He would have been better off spending a year as a gambler on a steam boat.

Wallis bathed with warm water for the first time since he could remember, freshened and wiped his gear as best he could and stepped down for breakfast. Not being a horseback rider, he wore no spurs and he barely squeaked the boards on the steps as he walked down to the breakfast and main hall of Le Pondemour. The hall had a bar along one end, facing the swinging doors of the entrance, in between there were around twelve round stone topped tables each with four chairs. Most of the tables were occupied by early breakfasters, with coffee, buttered bread slices (more like chunks) eggs, sausage, beans on the tables. Everybody looked busy, some of the tables had just two or three, and a few even just one guest. There must have been around thirty five or forty people at the tables many of them talking in between eating. Nobody was particularly well dressed, they all seemed to be in clean, but working clothes, with only one gent more formally dressed in waist coat, top hat on the chair beside him and a short tie with a clean, silk looking shirt. He seemed to be only on beans, bread and coffee, some biscuits. And he was carrying a colt still strapped around his waist belt in a well-oiled looking holster.

Wallis reached the bottom of the stairs and looked around to choose a vacant table. That was when the gent in the waist coat pushed back his chair and standing up, stepped forward. 'Want some breakfast, do you? He asked sardonically 'Finished with shooting defenseless, hardworking Africans? Wallis measured him and by way of introduction stuck out his hand 'JW Wallis' he said quietly 'and I don't remember shooting any defenseless people, African or not'. 'From Texas are you? queried the man, ignoring the outstretched hand 'They call me Bacon, I'm from Batesville'. 'That Bacon' Wallis exclaimed softly 'the Bacon I know is wanted in Batesville, Crystal City, Asherton and Carrizo Springs'.

'Hardly the complete list' Bacon smiled thinly moving forward till he stood parallel to the far end of the bar. Behind him was a dark piano against the wall, probably used in the evenings. Wallis was now directly facing Bacon, less than twenty feet away.

'So, what's the racket here? Wallis asked. 'Well, my friends in Batesville, Asherton and Quemado let out the big secret of Solomon's mines, nice folks like you come down looking. Cuamba and Luiga relieve them of their worldly possessions or take more money from them to give them directions to an elusive hoard of gold and precious stones' Bacon said smiling. 'Sorry about Cuamba and Luiga, they won't be troubling Texans any more' Wallis completed. Bacon stepped forward quickly, walking the half length of the bar to Wallis, his hand not near his gun. Bacon threw a punch, his right fist rocking Wallis, who stumbled into the room, against one of the empty chairs as he grabbed the chair and marble topped table for support. Wallis sat down abruptly on the empty chair, his right colt appearing quickly in his hand pointing dead centre at Bacon. 'Why don't you sit down' Wallis grimaced rubbing his painful chin. 'Don't mind if I do' Bacon replied pulling up another chair 'Show me how you are going to make it good'. 'Well, I came here looking for gold' Wallis smiled thinly 'Show me how and we will split it evenly'.

'Gold? Bacon replied thoughtfully 'There is the bank, a small amount in the Sheriff's office safe, the fortnightly coach from Meconta to Memba on the other side of Namapa. The coach has the most gold, with the weekly port wages, but is protected by four armed riders and one riding shotgun. Never been hit by outlaws. The bank is not so well protected and does not have much gold. The bank transfers daily surplus cash to Namapa. Namapa itself has enough guns to discourage the most hardened of outlaws'.

'I don't think you can help me much more' Wallis said thoughtfully. He looked around and the rest of the diners seemed happy to continue their breakfast. Some leaving and paying the bartender-cashier. The bartender himself was watching them but both his hands were on the bar, and he seemed merely interested. Wallis shot Bacon thrice rapidly, once in the gut and then twice in the chest. This was Africa. Montepuez did not have a Sheriff. 'Guess, I'll have my breakfast now' Wallis called out to the bartender-cashier 'Butterred toast, coffee and sausage for me…lots of butter please'.

A week later Wallis hit the bank on his own and took off on a customer's horse on the rail outside, with a small bag full of gold dust and coins, one largish biscuit. Three weeks later Wallis was sitting over a ledge, two rifles besides him. The coach's dust road ran below him between two ledges. This time Wallis needed help. He rode back closer to the Messalo on the way to Marrupa – the bunch of boulders which faced the thick line of trees. The leopard family was thankfully lazing on, and around the tree, their original lookout post. Wallis waited and eventually two, no, three Africans walked out of the tree line. An hour later, Wallis had convinced them, to support his taking of the coach, for a share in the gold. Chemba, the leader of this little team frowned 'We will take one third of whatever we take'. 'Ok' Wallis said, putting out his hand grandly to shake on the deal.

While Wallis waited on his ledge, the Africans waited down below around the corner with their spears and long knives. Wallis was to provide them with cover from above. Everything went wrong for the Africans from the beginning. As the coach rounded the bend, Wallis shot the man riding shotgun, then fired two shots into the four stage horses. The stage came to plunging horse-screaming tumbling halt. The riders behind pulled up sharply. The Africans stepped out in front of the stage coach, not sure what to do. The riders rode out front, assumed that Chemba had attacked the stage and opened fire. The three African warriors were shot down by a hail of rifle and colt lead. They were cut down and hardly knew what had happened, still confidently expecting covering fire from above.

Wallis then opened fire on the exposed riders. They were closely bunched and Wallis let loose with both Winchesters, a hail of bullets on the plunging riders. One rider tried to make it to cover and Wallis merely shifted the angle of his Winchester. Within minutes, Wallis had emptied his Winchesters, the scene below was of screaming horses and eight dead men – four coach riders, three Africans and the coach shotgun rider. Wallis calmly reloaded one Winchester with four rounds, then shot the coach driver who had been sitting by the side of the road. After putting away the wounded horses, Wallis finally stepped to the coach. One of the stage coach horses had not taken a bullet. The other horses were either down or had to be put down. The coach had two heavy strong boxes. Wallis shot the lock off both boxes. Both strong boxes were filled with neatly stacked gold coins and each box had a few sheets of tally and communication papers. Off the horses, Wallis picked four leather bags and filled these with gold coins. He put one bag on his horse and three on the coach horse. Then after a second thought, filled another saddle bag with gold coins and put this also on to the coach horse.

Wallis kept low, away from the roads, detoured to Meconta, avoiding both Namapa and then Memba. At Meconta he stopped only briefly, presenting a ragtag image, for supplies. From Meconta to Nampula was a shorter ride. At Nampula, he felt safer and stopped over for three days, trading in and changing horses. With fresh horses, Wallis reached Mocambique in good time. Now used to the haranguing needed for a boat or a passage, Wallis shipped out to Nacala, then to Quissanga, not having to stop over at Pemba. At Quissanga, Wallis discovered that he could move out from Quissanga itself as there was a ship scheduled to leave within the week, he did not have to travel further north to C Delgado and could skip Madagascar. Wallis played the part of a destitute but colt-toting Westerner quite well and that kept trouble away from him. He had discarded the long rifled Winchesters, carried the two colts and the short barreled shotgun. Months later Wallis was scheduled to return Port Lavaco, Matagorda.

If wishes were horses. After leaving Labito off the West of Africa, Wallis was stunned by Captain Mayoto 'We should be in England soon' Mayoto declared sucking on a dead cigar 'The weather looks good for the crossing'. 'England'!! exclaimed a stunned Wallis 'Why England?? I don't want to go to England. I'm headed for Lavaco'. 'Sorry, trade route change just before leaving' Mayoto said apologetically 'We're headed, depending on the draft either to Harwich, Felixstowe or Ipswich, though I would prefer, and know better the King's Lynn Docks or

Wells Harbour'. So it was that Wallis landed eventually at Ipswich. With many days on his hands, Wallis decided to stay back in England. England he reasoned was better than home at Eagle Pass, Spofford, Crystal City, Carrizo Springs or even San Antonio. England was quieter and safer for him, few questions would be asked about his time in Africa or the source of his wealth, and he could make up just about any story about his adventures in Africa and his source of wealth.

Two years later, Wallis was settled in the town of Diss off Attelborough. He had changed his identity, deposited his gold in a respectable bank, and was now Retd. Col. James Pearsall. Col Pearsall sat in a corner of the bar, smoking his cigar, comfortable in his tweeds, sipping his lager. There was a group of locals at the other end, gossiping about him, speculating about him. He didn't mind too much, there were mostly wary and scared of him. Missus Carlisle was holding forth 'Keeps guns, does he, was a great hunter and explorer. He's explored most of East Africa, left the army early because it was not active or violent enough. All in all, a man not to be trifled with. Funny though, shoots pheasants and foxes such as turn up on his estate, but keeps rabbits, hens and horses'. 'Drink a lot? Adam Cobworth queried. 'N'er more than he should' Misssus Carlisle retorted 'but I've seen him fooling around with cards and checkers by himself.

Wallis-Pearsall, stepped up to them, stood for a moment looking down silently at them, then turned and walked out. The air was crisp and fresh, yes, he thought, he had arrived. Norwich, King's Lynn Docks, Wells Harbour, Felixstowe, Ipswich and Harwich all had fortnightly payroll deliveries. It was only a matter of planning of detail, reasoned Wallis, after all, what was an active explorer to do in boring Diss off Norwich? From Norwich to Ipswich over land using the tramp cover. Then there were great luxury liners from Southampton to America. One to be launched in a few weeks was called the Titanic – real luxury, that was what he could afford to indulge in now. From New York he could go wherever he liked or back to Eagle Pass or

San Antonio, he might even take up as Sheriff of Spofford or Crystal City – yes, the Titanic sounded like his kind of passage. Crystal City sounded good, after all he had just disposed off Bacon, and unless he was mistaken he, himself was the only other bad guy around. Yes, he would book a ticket on the Titanic, and plan the easiest, most profitable, port payroll snatch.

Aloha Springs

He snorted and shook his head, flicking his hair across his damp forehead. With his left foot he drew small idle scratches in the dust. The sun beat down mercilessly, drying up the night's dew quickly. Nothing yet on the horizon, not a cloud, not a whisper of green, not a faint breeze of scent of water. A few hundred yards away, across a sunburnt rock, lay a huge lizard spread eagled, tongue flicking idly. He knew he could not go on much longer and the desert with its soft beckoning dunes of sand stretched lazily and unendingly before him. In the distance, maybe a hundred miles out was the mountain range. A range that promised water and shelter, a place to live, a place he could call his own.

He was not three years old when he had decided to leave. Bunched up with twenty or so others was not his idea of a life. Red Ralph and Rattlesnake Joe were fun sometimes, but it just wasn't enough. The plough was hard but the confinement was the worse of the two. He had often looked at the clouds and his spirit soared when he saw the eagles (or vultures?). He had been on the run for two whole days now, sure that the pursuit had dropped away. Red Ralph was the only one who could have caught him, but not burdened as he was, and besides he did not really want to catch up with him even though Rattlesnake Joe ran alongside to give him breaks. Maybe, he was just not worth the pursuit? Anyway, what mattered was here and now. His immediate problem was water. His second worry was the wolves. They managed to find him at night, always, sooner or later. He would have to make a break for the mountains without a rest, during the day. A hundred miles was possible, though it would take every ounce of strength, and some more. He had planned to do around forty miles in a day, but this was one last effort, once in the mountains, he could drink and rest at Aloha Springs at the base.

The soft whap of the bullet as it hit sand startled him. The bullet hit the cushion of sand about twenty five meters behind him. It seemed that Red Ralph knew that it was now or never. Once he started across the sands to the mountains, there would be no stopping him. Without bothering to look back, he slid down the dune, allowing gravity to work, using his legs as brakes. He landed at the bottom in a tangle of legs, stood up and then looked back. Red Ralph had not yet arrived at the top of the dune, so he had a running start.

He began his run or rather his quick shuffling walk, slowed, quickened, slowed yet again. Head down he ran into the sun, the soft sand making the going difficult. The mountains looked even further away, but the hint of mist at the foothills kept him going. His legs gave way and the mind drove him on. The mind gave way, and his spirit drove him on. No more drops of sweat, he was just too dry, merely thankful that he was not carrying somebody or anything else. Yet, he was making good time and the afternoon was nearing, the glow of the evening sun setting in. He would dearly have loved to take a break, but he knew that if he stopped he would not be able to go on. It was deliciously simple to lie down and sleep, but having left his friends behind he could not do that. Maybe one day, he would find a way to go back for them, to free them, to give them a taste of Aloha Springs.

He had first heard of Aloha Springs from the traveler. A weary, burdened, traveler who dragged himself into the station for a rest and a meal of beans, bread and sausage on the house. He had told them at night of the mountains, the spring, the desert, the vultures, the wolves, the shifting dunes, the starlit nights and the strange one branch, umbrella like tree that grew out of the sand. And then he was gone in the morning, heading into the city, to see the lights, make new friends, and maybe get a job. Rex had not forgotten and could not get it out of his mind. He wanted to find that stream, the spring, live in those mountains, too long had he lived outside the city, working the plough, looking after the chickens, giving the children rides. The run had been fun at first, tiring later and worrisome soon. He passed dried hides, piles of bones with the ribs sticking out like white fingers from the sand. But he believed the traveler, never doubted him for an instant, and wished the traveler a good job in the city.

The city was still a rough place. Unlike the farm, the city had some rough people. The city had those awful slaughter houses, racks of raw meat were hung out to dry and be sold. Drunks sometimes struggled through the main street, and worse, they tied their horses at the rails, away from the water trough, away from the grass. The stables were not much better, hot, dry places. One stable had even burnt down one night and there were four awful deaths. The jobs in the city were also not much better, hard work, low pay, little to eat and then discarded after you could not make the cut. The city had received a boost from the small mine nearby, but it was the farms that were the better places to work.

What had he been thinking?? Why on earth, did he leave the farm? Was it really worth it heading into the mountains? What if the mountains were equally sun baked and dry rock? What if the water had dried? What if the grass had long burnt to a dry cinder? Was the awful risk worth it?

To leave behind his friends, the farm, the chickens, the children, and Red Ralph. It was past four now and the sun was dropping, he dared to look up, heading in a straight line, the mountains still seemed a distance away, possibly another thirty (or forty?) miles away. The earth was firmer now, a sparse crop of rocks dotted the sand, making the going a bit easier. His throat was dry, his legs swollen, his shoulders ached and his head was positively baked, his forehead burned, his hair had long since become crisp and dried. He could do it, the risk was worth it, the springs and the good life ahead was his for the taking.

It was early morning the next day when he entered the foothills. He looked around him, sniffing the air, looking for some sign of cool breeze that would tell him where the water was. Rex smelt something awful. Surely not, not here. He walked in the opposite direction, slowly, trying not to make any sound of his clipped hooves on the stones. He soon came to a stream edge and drank his fill. The bank was covered in a thick carpet of juicy grass. This was the life!! Later in the afternoon, Rex trotted softly toward the awful smell. He looked carefully from between the thick leaves and closely set trees. The scene below shocked him to the core.

Rex stared as the butchers hacked away at the carcass of a horse, in fact two were hung up. They seemed to be separating the meat, the bones, the intestines, the hooves, the mane and even the skin. Blood dripping from the carcasses and two more horses tied down in a small corral, young wild colts. It was horrible. How could this be happening here? Thought Rex. Was nowhere safe? Rex neighed softly smelling the breeze and started carefully on the long way back to the farm.

It wasn't bad, ambition, but he had seen the world and home on the farm, was home, safe, secure, friends, family – well, at least until he could work for them at the farm.

Doctor Vince

Dr Vince was a tall, thin, white haired, bespectacled doctor. He was nearly always seen in his white coat. He had a clinic at Bristol. He had a couple of nurses and a receptionist who kept his diary. The clinic was roughly eight hundred neatly squared feet. It had his consultation room, a treatment room and a sort of clinic procedure room. Vince was happy. His practice was doing well. He saw on an average anywhere between seventy to a hundred patients a week. His nearest competitor Dr Herman, also a general practitioner, was around a hundred meters away, with a couple of pharmacies in between them. Herman was a good chap and a very good competitor – the sort who was not aggressively competitive and he could share notes with him on phone should the need arise.

Vince or Doc as his patients called him, had realized that barbers and doctors over time, learnt a great deal about their patients. Patients liked talking to their doctors, they assumed confidentiality and often talked to distract themselves while the doctor examined them or did a painful dressing on the foot or hand. It took Doc a few years of hard practice to realize that his patients, at least some of them, were making much more money than him. That made him unhappy. 'Rouffy' Vince called out to one of his nurses. Rouffy was a Malaysian, not more than five feet in height. He was ambidextrous, had worked earlier as a carpenter, house painter, plumber before training as a nurse. He was good with his hands, had a nice pleasing touch with patients, was very good at wound dressings, injections, and IV lines. Rouffy liked his work, gave him a sense of satisfaction and genuinely liked making his patients comfortable, he cared for the patients in a way that Vince never would.

'Rouffy' Vince continued now that Rouffy had stepped forward 'Im not in this evening for the evening run at five. If there is something you can do for a patient go ahead, if not reschedule for tomorrow. Let me know if something urgent turns up'. Vince took off his coat and walked out. The waiting room had just one patient a Mueller who needed a dressing changed on a cut on his hand. Mueller was quite happy for Rouffy to do it, especially now that Vince told him he wouldn't be charged. 'Meka' Vince called out to the other nurse 'you can take the evening off' and Vince was about to leave when he realized that Mueller had his dog with him.

 'Hey, Mueller, doggies not allowed in here'. Mueller stoically went on the defense 'He's hardly a dog, Doc, he's my live-in companion, fully insurable and tax deductible'. Vince shrugged and continued to walk out, he was not in the mood to discuss this with Mueller.

At six thirty, Vince was sitting in old Albert's café, with a coffee and a newspaper. Only he was trying to relax, neither reading the newspaper nor sipping the coffee. Vince watched the world go by and finally decided to amuse himself by leafing through the newspaper, the all interesting classified ads. A coincidence, he had just seen Mueller's dog Nix(on) and the classified ads seem to be full of ads for grooming, sale and treatment of pets, principally various breeds of dogs.

Meka joined Vince soon and sat directly opposite him 'throwing some more good money on coffee you will never drink? 'I'll drink this one if it makes you happy' Vince retorted 'every last drop. 'Don't bother' Meka said still looking generally happy 'When are you going to get this medical practice of yours, working in serious money? Plastic surgeons, orthos, gynaecs all make tons of money. Why, Vince, I bet the nearest undertaker takes in more than you and he just puts them under'. Vince looked thoughtful 'I'm working on it, Meka, patience, Herman has some ideas'. Meka was an Indian nurse, an immigrant to the country with a supposed husband. They divorced promptly within months of Meka entering the country. 'Hermaan has some ideas?? Meka half yelled between her teeth 'when are you going to realize that Herman is developing his practice and fishing to see what investment money he can take in from you, to combine both the practices. Herman has an ortho in his clinic and x ray equipment. You have zilch. The only thing keeping you going is that you work mornings in addition to the evening five through eight in the evening'. Vince smiled 'Well, not entirely Herman, I've got an idea myself, but it involves Rouffy'.

Meka was wary now. She knew that Rouffy was a better nurse than her and quite handy too. 'So, that's how it is? Meka stiffened. 'Nothing will change between us' Vince hastily put in, half sitting up in his chair. 'Coffee for you, Ma'am? the server finally turning up. 'Whatever' Meka waived him away and Mansfeld beat a hasty retreat. 'Let me explain' Vince started grandiosely. 'First off' Vince said 'we keep the morning timings, only you and me. 'And evenings? Meka was interested now. 'We schedule injury dressings, injection routines for the evening, and Rouffy can handle that pretty much on his own'. Vince explained 'anyways a lot of our patients prefer that'. 'And what are you and I supposed to do in the evenings? Meka sounded both wary and skeptical. 'We, my dear Meka, are going to open and run an evening pet shop and clinic. I am a GP, I can be a doggy GP so long as you handle the doggies.Lots of money in there' Vince carried on.

Meka looked furious 'Firstly, Vince, you clearly think that I am not good enough to change dressings and give injections. Secondly, I hate dogs, so go find somebody else to help you with the dogs'. 'Why don't you then take the evening shift then and let Rouffy and myself handle the pooches' Vince suggested. This was what he had always wanted but knew he could not put it across directly.'Hmph' muttered Meka, 'I somehow don't think you will make a lot of money, and besides you don't know anything about pooches'. So it was Doc Vince spent the next eight months at evening classes and examinations before qualifying as a veterinary doctor. Dobs Pooch Clinc opened with fanfare and fliers distributed at households and the local supermarkets (there were three) and at the few pubs around town.

Meka gave up on Doc Vince. Vince was not doing very well with the dogs and his GP practice was doing worse than ever. The patient flow in the evenings simply dried up as not many patients liked coming in to be managed by Meka for regular medications, dressings and injections. Doc Vince replaced Meka by a local recruit, actually, sticking a notice in the window of Dobs Pooch Clinic. Sheila was a middle aged, nurse who had retired from a hospital after fifteen years and was quite happy helping out with dogs in the evenings for three hours. Sheila had friends and knew where to distribute the fliers and wanted Vince to be successful. She simply liked animals and did not like Vince losing money on the pet clinic. So it was that Sheila distributed fliers at the Bristol Museum & Art Gallery, Clifton Bridge, Clifton Down, the hippodrome, and as far afield as Spike Island, Cotham, St Andrew's Park, and Montpelier. Vince and nurse assistant Sheila soon had more pets coming in than they could cope with. Herman got one of his old friends an elderly, miserly Doc Vaughn to take pets in the morning, pets other than dogs, including mainly cats, the odd bird, a few children's hamsters and even the occasional goat. Although, Vaughn could do nothing really for birds and hamsters, he was quite firm and competent with pet kitties and adult cats.

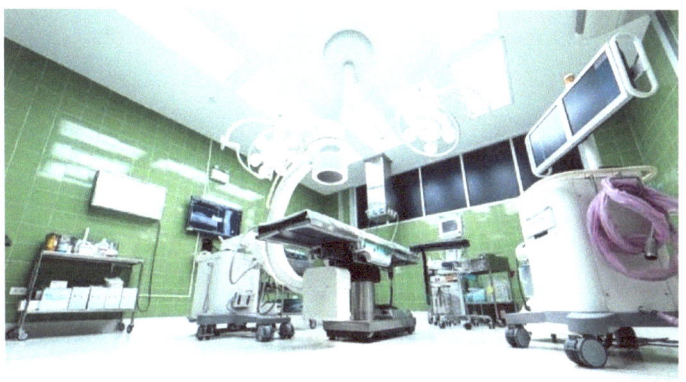

Doc Vince was finally really busy but not making big money. His ambition after all, was to become rich and not just to keep himself busy ten hours a day. Doc Vince, one fine Monday evening was treating a hound for a sprained right foreleg, no broken bone, simply a strain. McMaster was the dog's owner and the dog was named Cavery. Cavery was a good, well behaved three year old. McMaster was delighted with the progress made by Cavery over the next five days. Vince was a little surprised 'Don't mind if I ask you, McMaster, but what is it that you find quite so adorable about Cavvy here? He's an ordinary looking mutt, if ever there was one, only well behaved'.

'He's a CHAMP' McMaster roared fondly 'a champ he is. He's not finished off the board in seven races so far and has won five. Bought him as a pup for all of a thousand pounds and in seven races, prize money and bets included, he's given me fifteen thousand six hundred pounds. You've done a good job with him, should be back on his feet in the races soon. I was worried I would have to ask you to put him down if his limp continued'. Vince screwed up his forehead 'over fifteen thousand pounds in seven races? How many would he run eventually' 'Oh, about thirty before we get him to a breeder, I would say he can finish at sixty to seventy five thousand pounds'.

That did it for Vince. He became a specialist in treating greyhound racing dogs.

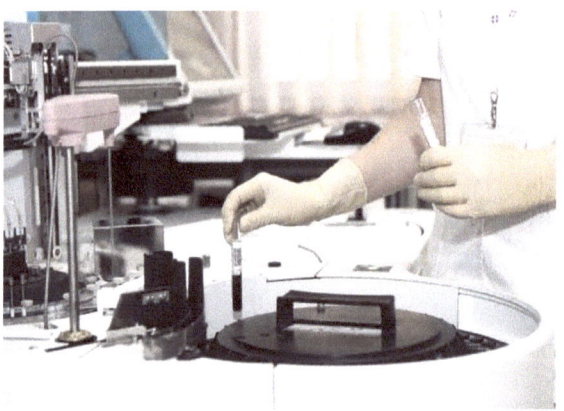

He marketed his clinic at the Swindon races and as far as Poole. Gloucestershire nearby was also good although prize hounds were few there. Once a month, Vince went down to Burnham by the sea and practiced there. He had a simple model for the towns. Appointments in advance by calling the Dobs Pooch Clinic at Bristol. Depending on the requests, Vince took a full day on weekends for dogs, or sometimes did the morning as a GP and the afternoons as a veterinarian, returning late evening, driving back. Vince enjoyed coffee at Costa at Burnham, Bristol and Gloucester, enjoying the strong blend. It was through McMaster, Cavvy and Swindon that Vince really hit the jackpot. He had concocted a small injection stimulant which made Cavvy an even better race runner little soup up before a race. Cavvy's fame brought in Zerco Frances, a Greek of mixed heritage who had at any time three of four greyhounds and paid really well. Herman was by now left far behind looking after talking parrots, pet rabbits and the like. The money in greyhound treatments and booster shots was of course in the betting, rather than the prize money. So it was that Vince appointed Noel, an immigrant from an island in the Philippines to handle the placing of bets for Dobs Pooch Clinic, all legal and above board. Vince now had an open top Beamer, was free of Meka and had a flourishing practice which he could sell at a high valuation.

So, it came about that Sheila, Vince, Rouffy and Noel were having afternoon tea on a Sunday with McMaster and Cavvy, now retired and laying down at the foot of the table, as they say outside. It was Sheila who first raised the issue 'Doc, while the going is good, can't we sell the clinic the stimulant souped up injections and cash in? Make all five of us rich? 'But then what do we do? That's all very well for you, McMaster and Cavvy, but what are Noel, Doc Vince, and myself to do after that? Rouffy asked, sounding just a little irritated. 'I'll come with you' Sheila put in quickly, help you set up, be your partner'. While the rest looked mystified, Sheila explained 'It's a question of getting the dosage sizes right' she explained, still not leaving the others puzzled and now more than slightly irritated. But it was a close dose team and they liked each other, especially Cavvy and McMaster.

So, eventually, in a few months, Dobs Pooch Clinic changed hands. Dobs was now wholly owned by Doc Herman who took on a couple of more partners. MCVSRN was incorporated as a company in Kentucky. The five of them moved to the USA, first enjoying a modest traveling holiday. At Kentucky, Vince, fine-tuned the dosages on thoroughbred horses at the stable, being trained as two year olds for the racing season ahead. Horse owners trusted the foreign, old money, European sounding name. Vince tried out his mix on really good racing horses, and got good results. The results were really good even without using banned anabolic steroids. In just four years, MCVSRN had wins at the Belmont and Preakness. Strangely, Vince's formulas did not help over the shorter distances and they could not bring into the winner's circle a horse for the Kentucky Derby.

Sheila eventually retired a very rich lady at the age of 65 and enjoyed traveling on cruises, taking in a bit of salt water golf. Rouffy became an expert thoroughbred appraiser, tipping investors on purchases from breeders, Noel was his business partner. Both of them had seaside villas, enjoyed hunting season, golf and river rafting. Cavvy had died, Rouffy now had two greyhounds. McMaster was content to retire. He took up an apartment in Manhattan on 34th and 8th opposite 1 Penn Plaza. McMaster, now without the benefit of Cavvy's company, spent his time window shopping in Manhattan, curiously observing the tourists and having meals at the Ramada opposite 1 Penn Plaza. He loved the concept of twenty four hour diners and took a fondness to bacon and corned beef.

Doc Vince married twice, once at Harris County, Fort Bend and then at Jacksonville, Florida. Both beautiful ceremonies, the lawful registrar being in both cases Noel. Vince liked the ceremonies and the locales and inviting friends for the festivities. He protected himself each time with agreements. He also then divorced twice and acquired a home by taking over a small island off Antigua and Barbuda. He was at ease with the local inhabitants, and they spoke good English, some of the nearby islands actually being British territories. Once a year they met, having sponsored a seniors golf tournament in Florida. The first edition of the Cavvy-MCVSRN Golf tourney was held in 1976 with ball collection on the course managed by trained greyhounds. Vince, eventually, did win the Kentucky Derby for a trainer, but only because of an error as the horse was given a double dose of his stimulant, the groomer not knowing that the first dose had been given the previous evening by a vet going on leave on race day. Talk about coincidences, the colt's name was Mekah.

Marrupa

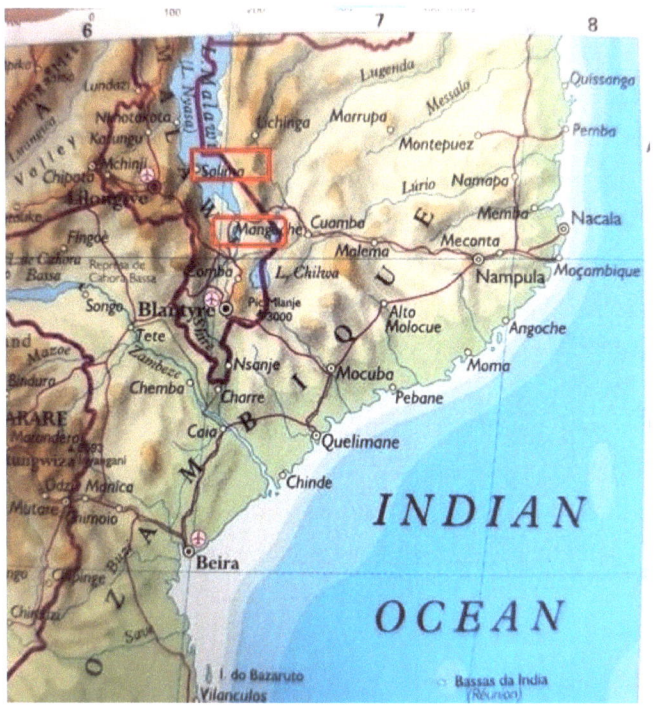

I wish I'd been there earlier. It might have made all the difference. So all I can tell you is why he was murdered. Doc Moroni was the world's foremost climate change scientist at the time of his death. He was also a researcher and inventor par excellence, there are key differences for not all scientists are researchers or inventors as I knew only too well as a scientist without a single patent to my name. Moroni was twice nominated for prestigious international awards and had refused. Awards meant nothing to him, his motivation was money. He was, had been, a thin gaunt man, white haired at a young age, never known to have a sense of humor. And, yet, Moroni was a kind man, who was known to have helped local communities with projects such as water conservation, waste management, preservation of village arts, and education of adults and children at villages within his reach. Doc Moroni had a beautiful handwriting, a good voice and was patient as a teacher, he really liked to teach and believed that Africa could be a wonderful continent, not just for wild life or tourists. He believed in the unification of Africa fractured by the British and French across tribes. Moroni had never married, however, he had a son Toumaas. Toumaas did not push the envelope on his father but worked closely with him, helping him in his research.

At the time of his murder Dr. Moroni was sixty eight. He had a substantial laboratory and research facility in Mozambique, funded in part for the past few years through my efforts. He had chosen to live in Mozambique although it was said he was born in Bulawayo, Zimbabwe. I first met Moroni as the team leader of a visiting delegation from the United Nations Technology Development Council (UNTDC). The UNTDC was, at the time, a highly secretive agency of the United Nations, supported only by the MI5, CIA, Knesset, RAW and NSA. The UNTDC's role was to identify early stage advanced technology development which could be useful in improving environmental conditions. Waste management, energy conservation, solar power, energy from non-fossil fuel resources were key focus areas. For years, UNTDC had fought the big six automotive majors, pushing for them to develop a few of the many alternatives to the cylinder-block engines. The technology had been there for over fifty years, however, the big six had bought patents and stowed them away. Similarly, the warp technology fueled by an ocean bed chemical which the Japanese had discovered, had been effectively shelved by jet engine aircraft manufacturers and warp flight was labeled as unreliable and more risky than the Concorde.

I stood hesitantly in the meeting room. It was a room for just six persons, so calling it a conference room would have been out of place, neat and cream like a hospital consultation room. I held out my hand warmly

'Very happy to meet you again Dr. Moroni. There is so much you could tell us, and we hope to be able to help you'. 'Help me? I don't think I need help' Moroni muttered in response, ignored my outstretched hand, walked quickly to the other side of the room and sat himself down. I sat down awkwardly. Moroni waited, not speaking. A tall, heavy set African youngster, probably in this twenties entered the room. He did not introduce himself. As we walked in, Moroni spoke 'Toumaas, will you please offer and help these gentlemen with some tea? I'm sorry we do not serve coffee'. After a few brief exchanges, Toumass neatly placed cups of green tea without sugar or honey before the three of us from UNTDC. 'So, how is Uncle? Moroni started off. He liked to call UNTDC as Uncle. Uncle had funded Doc Moroni to the extent of over ten million United States dollars in the previous year and we needed to put together a progress report to support the current year's funding request.

'What is your current year's funding request? I came to the point directly. This was a very intelligent man and there was no point in running around the bush. The USA had supported Doc Moroni's research despite the President having a declared cynical attitude toward such research in general. A President, who half believed that global warming could even benefit humanity and at worst was a hoax put out by South East Asian countries who continued to raise coal based power plants instead of growing more crops.

'We need a bit more this year as we need to produce prototypes. We have a few streams of technology and will have to prepare around fifteen prototypes to prove concept. This year we need total funding of an estimated sixty million and the next year around hundred and fifty' Moroni briefly said, quickly and with no further detail. He did not have the customary two identical application folders before him, therefore, he was not prepared to give more information. I was instantly alerted and worried. Alerted that this meeting was not going as usual, this was the third year I was meeting with him. Worried because Doc Moroni would not be talking aggressively, unless he already had a commitment from a private sector company or a communist government or a rogue government, a political outcast, sanctioned government.

Moroni was an energy conservationist at heart and in his veins. An arterial veinous fistula would not have worked in his case, he would have energy conservation flowing both ways. However, he did not believe in animal conservation. His personal office, I had discovered on my first visit, had the heads of a lion, a zebra and wildebeest mounted on the wall, personally shot by him, the lion at fairly close range. His laboratory and research facilities were at Marrupa off the Messalo river, and at Namapa close to the port Memba. Memba had a small airport on the outskirts with a sand cleared runway long enough for propeller driven single engines. From Namapa we had proceeded to Marrupa across the almost now dry bed of the Messalo. The Messalo ran dry for a good part of the year but was known to flash flood often during the monsoon. It took us five days to reach the research building, we were transported in a stumbling, ambling convoy of mules, donkey and two camels. The research facility was a domed structure, long, almost like a greenhouse from the outside. One end connected to the adjoining hill and through and opening disappeared into the hill. The opening into the hill was dark and unlit, a single narrow gauge rail track leading off into the hill through the opening. Moroni was not particularly neat or fastidious. The surrounding was scattered with uncared for shrubs, discarded shovels, barrows and a couple of earth movers which had not been used in a while. A couple of mules grazed nearby, their ropes trailing.

'You're asking for a commitment of two hundred and ten million? I asked quietly 'After all the support we have given you...'my voice trailed off. 'Two hundred and ten million for two years' Moroni corrected 'I could then sell you the technology. Even a big game hunter like me needs to retire'.

'Retire? I asked, this was getting serious 'You have a breakthrough then? You are satisfied enough to move to prototypes? 'I would say so' Moroni replied a bit smugly. I was genuinely worried now. It seemed that Moroni did not care whether UNTDC came up with the money or not.

In fact his whole attitude indicated that he did not want UNTDC to pay him his funding requirement, maybe it was deliberately over stated. My two member team at the table was of no use, they were tough guys, secret service protection, the original kill bill squad, the type who could give Quentin Tarantino nightmares. The decision was mine, the failure was mine. We had not kept close enough tabs on Moroni, we had not been monitoring his communications and e mail. 'You know we will need more detail Dr. Moroni' I said feebly but firmly. There was a minute of silence and then Moroni said 'Very well, I will explain myself. You do know I like wild life photography and big game hunting. I only hunt in areas which are clearly over stocked and need an element of culling. Never for ivory and all the meat is given to the villagers. Although, I do not really prefer Zimbabwe, the wild life there meets my requirements and I do not require a permit or worry about rangers.

Last year I took a small expedition accompanied by my son Toumaas, into the Mateke Hills. We were disappointed as there was only a thin fringe of big game and the hills were mostly dry with few water sources. Regrouping, Toumaas returned to Marrupa, whereas I decided to extend my holiday and refresh myself. We continued past Gwanda into the Matopo Hills. The hills there were lush green, a paradise and although there was no big game, we took excellent shots of big apes and orangutans, some beautifully colored birds.

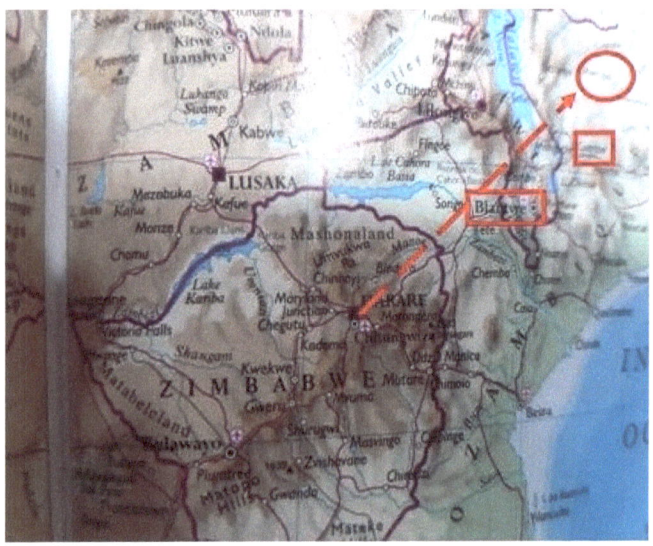

After a week, we returned to Marrupa. I was tired and on the return used the propeller aircraft which you so kindly funded. So our return journey was via Bulawayo, Chitungwiza, Blantyre, an unknown landing strip at Cuamba before flying to Marrupa. Quite scenic and very uneventful. I returned a refreshed man, full of vigour.

In the months following my return, I plunged myself into my work, using, I am afraid, a whole year's funding and resources in just a few months. But I had my breakthroughs' Moroni said with a satisfied look. 'Wait, breakthroughs? I interrupted 'more than one? This could help the funding case' I was excited. Moroni looked disinterested and did not apparently share my enthusiasm. Toumass cut in as Moroni sipped his cold green tea 'Yes, two key breakthroughs. The first an advanced process for harnessing solar power, storing and distributing the power using nothing more than sand packed in trays as conductors and storage batteries. The cost of such power would be a sixth of conventional sources. The second, is connected to the first in a way. Using solar power, and allied processes, an integrated module of efficient desalination has been constructed. Given Africa's and Asia's sea shores, that would end the water problems in these two continents, and the power shortages in a major way' Moroni stepped in 'As you know, I employ researchers of many nationalities. I wanted to discover value. I received offers from, as expected China. North Korea and one of the Middle Eastern Gulf countries. In Africa, I received offers from the Umvuke and Kapaeta industrial groups, they were clearly backed by some politicians. China has made the best offer and the next best offer is from the Middle East (I realized later that it was a joint offer from the Gulf Cooperation Council countries. Their interest, apart from the obvious uses, was whether the system could be weaponized). I was offered, in addition to various sums of money, a research facility on Mars for my use. There I realized that the China, North Korea was a joint bid supported by Iran and Pakistan. So, you see, it has become quite complicated.

We decided on a break out and huddled, trying to decide how to manage Mr. 'Mars', the erstwhile Dr. Moroni who seemed to have solved one heck of a major Rubik cube on the energy and water problems of Asia and Africa. After lunch we regrouped with Doc and

Toumaas in the meeting room. We sat glumly looking at each other. 'Some more tea to help us through? The UNTDC man on my left said 'my turn now to serve you all'. We had our tea and started talking shop about the weather, the people and the animals. In five minutes, Dr.Moroni and his son Toumass were both either dead or seriously dying. 'Never liked green tea, especially without mint and honey' I said. We sprinted out of the room to the gate past a couple of surprised guards. The man from UNTDC, Moroni's 'Uncle' pulled something small out of his pocket, called in something to somebody at the other end. We were soon on our way, Uncle's man had called in a massive air strike to destroy the entire facility at Marrupa and also Namapa. A day later we were sitting around a coffee table at the port of Memba.

It was seven in the evening, we were quiet, it was hot and sticky with humidity and flies. There were quite a few people about and in the restaurant. Some drinking, but most eating and drinking. 'We did not have a choice.' Songae said 'There was simply nothing else we could have done. And besides' Songae smiled here.'I think he was foolish to trust me just because I was originally from Zimbabwe and he knew that none of us liked his green tea from the last visit. In fact I am really sorry that you, Doc Welsh do not have either tea or coffee'. 'I never have tea or coffee Sonny' I said quietly, now suddenly alert. 'More's the pity, Doc, happy hunting in the Matupo Hills'. He pulled a pistol then and tried to shoot me under the table. I had him covered from the moment we sat down. I was an environment scientist all right but had been seriously trained by MI5. I shot him under the table twice in the gut and he slumped, in his chair, almost grateful, looking a bit apologetic, groaning as he fell. As a reflex, he fired a shot into the base of the wooden table. It was a thick table and the bullet did not go through, broke off and a fragment hit me in the thigh. I hobbled away. Two weeks later I was recovering at a hospital in Burnley off Blackburn. I received in the evening a small package, with some flowers, mint, wild honey, green tea and a card thanking me in the dearest terms for my recent services. The Chinese always thanked me for services rendered. Somewhere in the Caribbean, my hurricane bank account would be a good bit heavier.

CHGT

Jeremy was a lawyer. He was a specialist in corporate law and intellectual property including trade-marks, patents and brands. UNTDC 'Uncle' had sometimes referred matters to him as an expert on patents. There were situations that called for legal resolutions of matters instead of a more traditional, lower cost bullet. The United Nations Technology Development Council was a highly secretive organization funded by the Security Council members, to track, acquire and in some cases destroy technologies that were ahead of human development and interest. Some technologies UNTDC had acquired or destroyed as policy, included obtaining minerals from the Moon, warp flight for aircraft and spacecraft, advanced robotics, energy sources other than fossil fuels, waste to fuel generation etc.

Jeremy was of medium built, had a shock of thick black hair and was always impeccably dressed in Blue Cross suits. No blazers or jackets for him. He had a slight sense of humor and was excellent at communications and relationship management. A good lawyer. A great candidate for the role of the handsome Count Dracula, except for the incisors. He could have been an excellent dentist too, his clients never felt the pain. I had to visit Jeremy and his associate Adam Priestley (his nick at office was 'Bishop' or just 'Bish') in connection with an inconvenient matter that had risen recently and urgently in India. Apart from being good with patent law generally, Jeremy was a good man to discuss legal strategy with. I met with Jeremy and Bish at their offices at Plimsbury Square, up a littls slope at literally a square. After being ushered into the meeting rooms overlooking a fountain and a little garden, I sipped my customary green tea with mint and honey which Bish had quickly arranged, along with sparkling water and some butter chocolate cookies. Walking around in London was a thirsty business these days, at least for me.

'What brings you here Denis? Jeremy asked. He was never one to talk shop but not formal. Simply conscious of everybody's time. Bish was a thin, sharp looking associate. We had background checked him as well. He lived alone and his landlady perpetually worried that he did not eat well enough and plied him with heavy mash and steak dinners, apart from huge breakfasts. Jeremy lived in the city during the week and retired to his home on Saturday afternoons, at Basingstoke. A charming tiled house, very comfortable, family and Labrador to go. I noticed that since we last met, Bish had grown a bit around the waist, obviously no longer being able to fend off the landlady's mash, steak and Olympic size breakfasts. Her Olympic breakfasts included the works – cream & honey pancakes, baked beans, hash brown, sautéed mushroom, roast tomato, Cumberland sausage, toast and coffee to wash down. Strong black coffee you could float a horseshoe, or at least pony shoe on. Aunt Violet Wilma (the landlady – at Uncle we simply called her VW) looked after Bish and suspected he worked at something terribly important in the city.

Bish never took to his accomodations any files or case of papers or folders. He relaxed with music, preferring a classical gramophone and a very large collection of technical and fiction books. VW often complained to him that he was turning her accomodations into a large library. Bish never had any visitors. Jeremy Hooper lived equally anonymously in the city. Jeremy cycled to office, wearing protective gear, helmet, knee and elbow guard. He showered and changed at the office. The cycle ride each way was his exercise and he did a bit of swimming on Sundays. Jeremy lived at a perfectly quiet, indistinguishable house about half way between Watford and London. It was a house without a Labrador or a terrier, no doggy hair on his suits.

'A little matter concerning a development in India, Jeremy' I began 'A few months back I was called to our office in Bombay ('Mumbai, now, isn't it? Bish interrupted) to discuss a matter. One of their industrialists facing a mountain of debt on which he had defaulted, had come up with a very interesting piece of collateral'. 'India, you do get around Denis' Jeremy said 'The land of snake charmers, rope tricks, Taj Mahal and masses of poor people in the midst of riches'. 'You are closer to the truth than you can imagine, Jeremy' I said. 'Karthik owes the public sector banks billions. He had borrowed for two large integrated steel plants, a low cost airline, a luxurious yacht, an interest in racing thoroughbred horses, an interest in Formula 1 racing, an old palace converted into a super luxury hotel and a small island somewhere near Seychelles. The problem of course being that not much of this turns out any cash profit and the borrowings keep climbing. His lifestyle of course does not help matters. He has it seems spirited away a good amount of money to London'.

'Collateral' Jeremy said thoughtfully 'Tangible or intangible? It would have to be something extraordinarily valuable to cover billions'. 'That's just it, Jeremy' I replied 'I don't know yet what the collateral is, only that is an invention, something that any government or organization would pay billions of dollars to get hold of, at least that's what Karthik claims'. 'Tell us more about Karthik' Bish said.' Heavy set, French beard, open necked shirts, gold chains, gold bracelets, not tall, five-five, arrogant, huge risk taker, great fondness for luxuries and soft living' I filled in 'He has given us a laptop with a password and once we get in, he will phone in a string of numbers to key in. All very mysterious, but that it the only way he is willing to deal these cards. We could of course pull the plug on the whole show, and the banks then would need to write off tens of millions of dollars'. 'Our meeting rooms are not really the best place for this, Denis' Jeremy said quietly' we are on camera and voice recorder here all the time'. 'Let's use Aunt Wilma's study' Bish said and we agreed as there did not appear to be any risks there. VW was happy enough to see us, happy to see that Bish was meeting with important gentlemen. VW quickly came up with tea, creamy scones and cookies, though I would have preferred a chilled pint of beer.

When we had tucked into the scones and cookies, I finally opened up the laptop, half expecting something to jump out of it. The password prompt came up and I called Karthik. 'CHGT' Karthik said straightaway, expecting me to ask for the password, not even waiting for my question 'all in caps, Denis' Karthik added. He sounded calm but serious, this was obviously no joke or prank. The laptop screen had now several icons, one named CHGT. He asked me to click on the icon and it asked for a number. Karthik carefully read out a number to me, a nine digit number, almost like a GPS coordinate or a latitude longitude address. I keyed in the number after writing it down carefully on one of Aunt Wilma's thoughtfully provided napkins.

There was a buzzing sound, like an electrical disturbance, then a wave of bluish, but transparent light, flickering, and then gradually taking shape. And there was Karthik sitting in the vacant chair at the table, smiling smugly. The three of us were shocked, truly shocked. 'Teleportation? Jeremy asked raising his eyebrows 'What's with the CHGT and the numbers? 'Karthik laughed uproariously, his whole frame shaking 'CHGT is the project code, simply meaning Come Here, Go There' for my teleportation machine!! The numbers are the unique identification code for myself, after having scanned myself at the place of origin. What you have is about a third of the machine or technology. Waive my loans and you will get the package. By the way, the Indian scientists had named it IAUJ – idhar aao, udhar jaao, but to globalize it I switched to the translated CHGT'. 'Explain!!' I demanded 'how does it work?

'Simple, my dear Watson' Karthik said ' I scan the object or person by a machine at the source, obtain a sequence of coded numbers and this can then be downloaded by the software at any location on this planet. Any object, any person, any animal, any size'. The three of us stared shocked at Karthik. 'That's my first collateral' Karthik grinned 'I am a sort of collector. The second device uses solar energy to obtain water from the atmosphere – can be used anywhere, can be scaled to any capacity, will solve water shortages and also can deconstruct the eye of a hurricane – interested? We continued to gawk, stare at him, not fully comprehending and still not fully believing that Karthik was sitting at our table. 'Give me a few minutes, let me think this through Karthik' I finally blurted 'you understand, that these are stunning developments? 'Sure, take your time, I'm not going anywhere – for now' Karthik laughed again loudly while tucking into my scones and cookies. He even helped himself to green tea, mint and honey using a spare cup from the side board.

While I sat thinking, Jeremy and Bish spoke to each other in low tones. I started playing around with the laptop, clicked an icon and the laptop took a picture of the table startling us with the quick flash. 'Hey, watch what you're doing with that' Karthik said agitatedly. I clicked twice again and there was the now familiar buzzing, bluish flash and Karthik disappeared from the chair.

Jeremy and Bish both stared transfixed at the chair, then at me. 'Simple, my dear Hastings' I grinned 'I fed in the coordinate numbers of the table and transported Karthik into the table, his own coordinates already being in the laptop. Do we have a utility man here? Could you please call him in here? A few minutes later, I had the borrowed tool box of a reluctant man in clean overalls. Once he had left, I picked out a hammer and a wrench with a firm handle. I first smashed the laptop. These Chinese made laptops had short lives but were hard to smash. I then unscrewed and smashed the table legs and broke the top into two. 'Jeremy, my friend, now you know why this meeting should have been held in your offices and not at VW's' I said smiling gently 'your partner's lounge has a perfectly good fireplace and this is just the weather for a nice, warm fire'.

There is the little matter of his outstanding loans' the lawyer in Jeremy kicked in. 'Oh, we will seize everything, yacht, villas, aircrafts, bank accounts, jewelry, palace, island, the works, write off the rest and get the central bank to print money for the shortfall'. 'Can he reappear? Bish asked thoughtfully. 'No Bish, not chance, you haven't seen the fireplace have you? I smiled 'Besides, I really, really do not like somebody turning up uninvited, drinking my green tea and eating my cream scones' I stepped out to call VW to request another serving, her cream scones were the best I had in a long time.

Horses

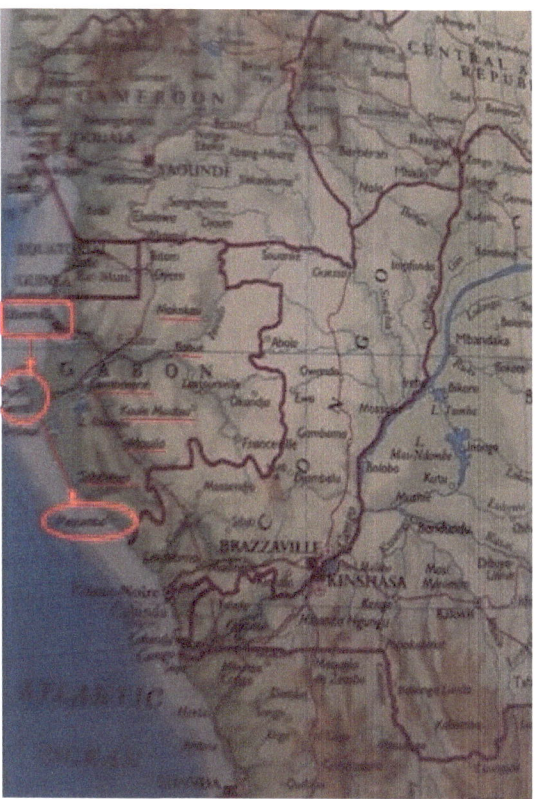

Wycombe was a medic. Wycombe had qualified as an orthopedic surgeon. Four years after working at a private hospital in Chelmsford, he decided to apply for the SAS, seeking more interesting life, not having family and not really expecting to qualify. The SAS was involved in counter terrorism, hostage rescue and covert reconnaissance, at the time. The special projects team of the SAS were specialists here, and included the counter revolutionary warfare [CRW] wing. Wycombe applied for a lark, a bet over a pint of lager. The SAS had just opened selection to the public instead of only service personnel. He aced the physical tests and the basic intelligence quotient, logic and strategic tests. The SAS had a unit called the 33 SAS. This unit was close to the prime-minister and the chief of army staff General Ashford Cusworth (half affectionately referred to as GAS).

33 SAS was set up to deal with heads of state removal strategies, and this was referred to by the acronym HORSES. Wycombe aced the sniper test as well, showing exceptional understanding of environments and positions, apart from great eyesight, hand and eye coordination. So it was that GAS approved the transfer of Wycombe to HORSES only a year after his commissioning. HORSES was involved principally in the Middle East, South America and the Far East. There were occasional forays when considered necessary in Africa.

Seth Wycombe was five eight, dark haired and of medium built. He had a strong frame with strong forearms and the legs of a heavy weight boxer having stood for hours in orthopedic operation theatres. Colonel James Davies called him in and tossing a thick folder at him explained 'A rare occasion to visit Africa, Wycombe, you will be accompanied by Major Corby. A little matter for the HORSES in Gabon. A personal request from GAS and the UN Secretary General' Davies grimaced 'UN? Wycombe asked raising an eyebrow. 'Yes, they have a sort of spy wing called UNTDC, short for United Nations technology development council'. 'Never heard of them' Wycombe commented drily 'And, please, who or where is Major Corby? 'Major Corby is a veteran of field operations in Afghanistan. He will watch your back. UNTDC will be represented by Davis Telford, he has been with them for a little over three years and was previously with the 4th Regiment'.

'What's with Gabon? Wycombe asked ignoring the folder. 'They have discovered, purely by chance a biological weapon, a weapon so potent that a very small quantity could end all life in a continent is a matter of weeks' Davies said quietly 'It's all in there'.

Wycombe was on the road to Gabon four days later with Corby. They would meet Denis Telford at Gabon, Denis was almost always to be found somewhere in Africa. Gabon was south of Equatorial Guinea and Cameroon, just north of Congo. Gabon has a land area of less than 105,000 sq. miles, and a population of only around a million. The official language was French, but almost everybody spoke either Fang, Myene or Nzebi. Gabon was interesting, it had reserves of petroleum and a small population. A den of corruption, amidst dwindling oil reserves. Wycombe and Corby reached the capital Lebreville and from there a uniformed troop took them almost like prisoners, by coast guard to Port Gentil and from there by road to Mayumba. The journey to Mayumba was by road in two black aircon, anonymous looking but very comfortable sedans. The thick seats and shock absorbers made them barely feel the dry mud highway. At Mayumba, Wycombe, Corby and Denis were put up in a luxurious hotel Le Pavillion where they were to meet the President Obame the next morning.

Presidente Obame was a large, smiling, genial lady, impeccably dressed and clearly superbly fit. Obame was a taekwondo champion and a national hero. She had become Gabon's fifth Presidente on the back of a popular uprising (all the uprisings at the time were popular). Obame was accompanied by the Governors of Mayumba, Port Gentil, Lambarene, and Ichubanga, all of whom were dressed in the traditional gabao cloak.

The Governor of Mayumba was in fact a pygmy, and the other two were from the Bantu tribe. All spoke their native languages, as well as French. Presidente Obame began when she was ready 'We are essentially a tribal society, gentlemen, interrupted occasionally, but not too frequently by colonial rule, the latest being the French. The only reason I am now Presidente is that we spend our budget now in turns each quarter on each of the Governorates, the ones here and the powerful ones at Lebreville, Koula Mouton, Mouila, Booue and Makokou. The Governor of Makokou is in fact the most recent recipient of our national largesse. But, come, everybody is happy, well at least till the oil at Grondin lasts' Obame sighed.

Denis looked at Obame 'When do you expect to run out? 'It's not a question of running out, the cost of production simply gets higher, the water production more, the quality lower, we net lower oil revenues. That is how the Governors of Booue and Makokou in particular began pushing for an alternative plan – they are so much younger' Obame sighed again, clearly not happy. Wycombe (the Gabonese had taken to calling him Why-comb-bay, which he kept unsuccessfully correcting) stepped in quickly, too quickly, lacking finesse 'So what's the alternative then, assuming that something has been put together that worries you Madame?

'The alternative, ah yes, the alternative' Obame replied quietly 'that is what we are here to discuss. Gabon currently has a per capita annual average income of around fifteen thousand dollars. We are hoping that the alternative will take this to closer to fifty thousand dollars Mr. Why-comb –bay'. Denis took over 'Yes, yes, of course, excellent, Madame Presidente, will you please tell you how, why and where we could be of assistance'. 'I haven't heard of you Mr. Telford or your UNTDC, so you must be secret service, which branch are you with, Telford? 'HORSES of the SAS' I replied not willing to explain more and Obame took HORSES to be the name of a regiment at the SAS.

The Governor of Ichubanga took up the narrative at this point, a thin man with a French beard 'You are aware of the great Komo river at the Libreville? For hundreds of years, the pygmy and the Bantu have lived at the banks of the Komo, venturing to fish and hunt as far down south as Ogooue and Onangue. We never did rely on oil, the French relied on oil and did not know how to live off the land. Now we go back to the secrets of the land'. Denis was tempted to tell him that oil came from the land, but he saw the point and held back. Corby was however, clearly getting impatient with all the humbug as he described it later. Corby called them bus conductor Governors, but then, Corby was an anarchist at heart, whereas Wycombe was merely a good sniper at heart. 'What's the big development then? Let's have it' Wycombe let fly, also a bit impatiently.

The Governor of Makoku smiled thinly (if it was possible for a stout man to smile thinly) 'You Europeans and Americans always do not want to waste the time? Eh? French, obviously being his preferred language 'The pygmy and Bantu both cautioned us against revealing anything to you'. Presidente Obame quickly added 'But we agreed, and therefore, this meeting. First our demands. We want a contract for the EU to purchase from us one million barrels of oil per day at the rate of thirty five united state dollars per barrel, for the next twenty years. We also want a down payment of fifteen billion dollars transferred to accounts of our choice'. While we swallowed that, Denis asked 'In exchange for what? You don't have one million barrels of oil per day to give us, at least not for twenty years'.

Obame said, very slowly and quietly 'You will assume that we will give you that quantity for twenty years, we will invoice you under bilateral agreement and you will pay. It is nothing but a simple deferred payment. We have two offerings. Please note that although the Governors are administrators, the pygmy, Bantu and Fang are the true owners. The first' She started dramatically 'producing a plastic packet in which there was sapling, the mouth of the packet was slightly open and the packet had a small quantity of soil and water in it as well. 'This little sapling, for years with the tribes, maybe a thousand years, grows and produces food when planted'. 'And...' Corby interrupted 'A lot of little saplings grow and produce food'. Wycombe looked uneasily at him, Corby was clearly on edge.

The Governor of Ichubanga, let it be said, shocked us with his reply, causing some involuntary jaw dropping on our side of the table 'In about four to six hours we could harvest, if we add a few drops of a very special berry mix to the soil'. Denis recovered the quickest 'And you have adequate supplies of both the sapling and the berry mix? Presidente Obame said 'We can produce as much as we want, Mr. Telford. There are two locations which have an abundant supply for the berry and the right climatic conditions. The area around Kinguele Falls, and at Lope National Park. 'Great' Denis returned 'So you have at least two alternate sources for the berry, one primary and another back up. What about the sapling? 'There also, we are rather fortunate' Governor Makukou chimed in 'At both Mount Milondo and Mount Bengoue, there are good supplies, Mount Bengoue is not far from the Republic of Congo, but the terrain is very difficult and a few well positioned troops can easily hold off a large force'. 'And' Governor Lambarene, who had been quiet so far 'we have a small but well equipped air force. Twin engine propeller aircraft, pilot agile at high altitude flying and landing, each aircraft capable of dropping barrel bombs and equipped with heavy machine guns'.

Presidente Obame looked at Bongo Moanda, her scientific advisor and then said 'The thing is not the fast growth to harvest maturity, the secret is how to stop the growth. If just two saplings were taken to America, given the right conditions and without our intervention, the entire North America would be covered in foliage in about two months' time, our computed models suggest'. 'Ah, so are we now talking terrorism, blackmail or both? Denis asked calmly 'since solving the food problem no longer seems the motivating factor? Bongo Moanda glibly said 'Probably, a bit of both and good intentioned food security. Of course we could also sell this to a whole number of countries such as Russia, China, North Korea, Iran or maybe all of them.

Wycombe thought morosely that HORSES was not equipped for this, taking out one Presidente was actionable, however, taking out a council of Governors looked decidedly improbable and a high risk venture. Denis was more experienced at this sort of thing 'Well, we do not have a quick solution, please allow us a couple of days to take some time off, and visit Lope National Park.

They politely adjourned after some small talk, about the weather in Gabon on the equator. The visit to Lope National Park was both exciting and boring. The park itself was boring, with little wild life except for a variety of birds during their visit. What was exciting was that they were followed by security at each step of the way and their night accommodation was clearly flooded with electronic surveillance equipment. Three days later, Major Corby had returned to England. Denis was no nearer to finding a solution and HORSES was reassigning Why-comb-bay to another spot of trouble, somewhere in North Africa. Denis was strolling around Libreville, humming a tune less song when the solution came to him. Window shopping apparently worked better for him at clearing the mind, than a trip to a national park.

The final terms of the agreement were amusing, if the whole matter was not so real. Two countries agreed to commit to development aid (primarily education, healthcare, power and roads) to the pygmy, Bantu and Fang. The area along the Komo river, Kinguele Falls and the Lope National Park would receive specific nature based scientific aid packages, designed to retain the pristine glory of these sites while improving accessibility for tourists. Major mining companies would help the development of the manganese, uranium, diamonds, gold and iron ore north east at Mekambo and Melinga.

The Grondin Oil revenues would be equally distributed personally amongst the Governors. In return, Denis secured a sign up that the Gabonese would no longer cultivate the sapling. Food requirements would be met through other crops and imports. Areas where the sapling was grown would be burnt to the ground under the guise of a civil war. Samples of the sapling would be given to NASA for introduction to Mars. The Gabonese, had in fact solved the problem of growing food on Mars.

Bongo Moanda joined up UNTDC. Presidents Obame after Sadaam, Gadaffi, Chavez, Putin, Erdogan, Mugabe, became another president for life. The Governors reaped huge ill-gotten gains from the Grondin oil field and invested over ninety percent of those gains in Germany, France, UK and USA in real estate. It took Equatorial Guinea and Cameroon only a few years to start border disputes. The Republic of Congo did not bother with border disputes, the Congolese led by Nguessou Jr. simply forayed across the border and took what they could.

Major Corby was happy as an anarchist for SAS in the Middle East, supported by a young social media expert. Denis acquired an assistant – Bongo Moanda. Wycombe became an instructor. His record stated that he had extensive experience in West Africa. He was a good instructor, his early students accounted for leaders such as Ndowe (bullet), Bujeba (car accident), Kwasio (fall from a cliff), and Mpongwe (crocodile). Africa was developing too fast and needed to be held back for the next century. After all nobody needed as yet, lions on Mars. Presidente Obame and her Governors agreed on this with UNTDC.

Ruster Keaton

I first met Ruster Keaton in early 2017. At the time, I was under anesthesia for an angiogram in preparation for clearing my blocked av fistula. Subsequently, in 2017, I had two more episodes of a blocked av fistula, cleared under anesthesia. I also had two surgeries under anesthesia on my feet (now partially amputated). During the sessions of pain, anesthesia and periods of immobile recovery in hospital, Ruster continued to relate his stories to me. He has a nice, calm style of telling the most aggressive stories. His descriptions are vivid allowing me to picture the events as they took place.

Ruster spends most of his time traveling the world. His adventures across five continents have enthused him to travel as much as possible on a shoe string budget. In fact, he once sold his only pair of shoes to pay for accommodation for the night. He is frugal and uses a  tube of toothpaste for example, for at least four months and never buys more than one pair of shoes or toothbrush in a year. Ruster has a ferocious appetite that is not partial to any particular type of food or cuisine. He once went three days without food in the mountains in Europe and then ate a whole lamb, roasted over a make-shift fire. Ruster is an excellent marksman and a superb horse rider. He is however, scared of heights and therefore shuns climbing. He rarely indulges in sports, not having the time for it, unless you call poker or roulette a sport. Ruster has so far emerged victorious in over a dozen pistol duels and numerous live cartridge Russian roulette pairs.

About the Author

Ruster Keaton is the pen name of Dr. Savio Gomes, for fiction stories which he writes occasionally. Savio is a consulting professional with a finance & economics background. He has travelled to Kenya, Australia, Italy, UK, USA, Thailand, Armenia, over 25 cities in India, Iraq, Iran, Saudi Arabia, Kuwait, UAE, Bahrain, Oman, Canada, Holland, and Turkey. Savio is also working on two more books, one encapsulating his experiences in consulting, and the other an updated treatise on economics including a collection of articles which were published in a newspaper. He completed his Bachelors of Commerce, chartered accountancy, certified internal auditor and certified public accountancy examinations whilst working and travelling. He lives in Kuwait with his wife Mallika and his two cats (Caramel and Dumpy, who in fact inspired one of the stories in this book).

Savio is also a rated FIDE chess player and participated in the world senior's chess championships in 2015 in Aqui Terme.